I have a boyfriend. . . .

"You know, I have a boyfriend," Summer said again. *I have a boyfriend who is sweet and wonderful and loves me to death and besides I'm spending spring break with him so what am I doing, pressing my thigh just the tiniest bit closer to yours?*

Austin was still looking at her when she finally met his eyes. "You have a boyfriend," he said very quietly. He was smiling, but only a little now. A wistful, sad, many-miles-away kind of smile.

"His name is Seth," Summer whispered, and then Austin touched her cheek and kissed her, soft and slow.

Don't miss the other books in this
romantic series:

#1 June Dreams
#2 July's Promise
#3 August Magic

Available from ARCHWAY Paperbacks

Summer

Spring Break Reunion

Katherine Applegate

AN ARCHWAY PAPERBACK
Published by POCKET BOOKS
New York London Toronto Sydney Tokyo Singapore

Tapp

This book is a work of fiction. Names, characters, places, and incidents are either products of the author's imagination or are used fictitiously. Any resemblance to actual events or locales or persons, living or dead, is entirely coincidental.

AN ARCHWAY PAPERBACK *Original*

An Archway Paperback published by
POCKET BOOKS, a division of Simon & Schuster Inc.
1230 Avenue of the Americas, New York, NY 10020

Produced by Daniel Weiss Associates, Inc., New York

Copyright © 1996 by Daniel Weiss Associates, Inc., and
Katherine Applegate

Cover art copyright © 1996 by Daniel Weiss Associates, Inc.

All rights reserved, including the right to reproduce
this book or portions thereof in any form whatsoever.
For information address Daniel Weiss Associates, Inc.,
33 West 17th Street, New York, NY 10011, or Pocket Books,
1230 Avenue of the Americas, New York, NY 10020.

ISBN: 0-671-51041-X

First Archway Paperback printing April 1996

10 9 8 7 6 5 4 3 2

AN ARCHWAY PAPERBACK and colophon are
registered trademarks of Simon & Schuster Inc.

Printed in the U.S.A.

IL 7+

1

Six Weeks till Spring Break, and She Doesn't Have a Thing to Wear

Eight juniors departments, thirty-seven bathing suits, and a half-dozen snarling salesladies into her quest, Summer Smith was ready to admit the obvious: She was a freak of nature.

In the overlit dressing room, four Summers stared back at her from full-length mirrors. They all looked somewhere between very dejected and totally annoyed.

Mounds of shimmering Lycra lay at her feet. Tanks. Thongs. Two-pieces. Suits for long torsos. Suits with inflatable boob enhancers. Suits with little tutulike skirts, like the ones mothers wore at the community pool. And then there were the suits that you would never in a gazillion years let your mother see you wearing, not if you ever wanted to leave the house again.

None of them was right.

Six weeks till the spring break to end all spring breaks, and Summer had nothing to wear to Florida.

Obviously there was only one solution. Nude beaches.

Right.

A clerk knocked on the door. "How are we doing in there?"

"We think maybe we should go to Alaska for spring break," the four Summers replied.

The clerk left with a sigh. Summer sighed, too. She was not a freak of nature. There was nothing wrong with her body. She liked her body just the way it was. Seth liked her body just the way it was. Maybe even a little *too* much.

Seth peered over the top of the door. "Want an unbiased male opinion?"

"Seth! Get out of here! They'll arrest you or something."

"There's no one in the dressing room but you. Besides, I'm going stir-crazy out there. You've got to buy something quick, Summer. I'm starting to sense some chemistry with one of the mannequins." He wiggled his eyebrows suggestively. "By the way, you look extremely excellent. Buy that one. Wear it home."

"It's February. It was sleeting on our way to the mall."

"So wear your mittens, too."

2

"You're no help. You're just a typical boy. As long as there's a lot of skin involved, you're okay with it."

"And that would be . . . wrong?"

Summer let out a long sigh. "What's the matter with me, Seth? Why can't I get my brain to function?"

"You're stressed out. That's why spring vacation was invented."

"But I'm a senior this year. We're not supposed to be stressed." She brightened. "Soon we'll have five days of complete bliss. It'll be just like last summer. No problems, no hassles. Sun. Sand. Surf."

"How about the fourth s word?"

"Sleep?"

"I was thinking about the one that ends in x."

Summer batted at him playfully. "I like a guy who's not afraid to dream."

She flipped through a bunch of suits on a hook. "It's between this black tank and that blue two-piece."

"The blue one. Definitely. *Now* can we go? My Egg McMuffin wore off hours ago."

"I need an objective *girl* opinion. I wish Marquez and Diana were here. I ought to call them."

"We'll be seeing them soon enough," Seth said flatly.

"Try to fake a little enthusiasm," Summer

3

chided. "We'll have plenty of time to ourselves over spring break. And Diana's the one who's snagging us the yacht. The rest of the spring breakers will be cramped in mildewy hotel rooms while we'll be living in the lap of luxury."

"I just wish I could have you all to myself," Seth said, gazing at her with a familiar look that was half lust, half love.

She stood on tiptoe, and they kissed over the top of the door. A harsh voice inquired, "And how are we doing in here *now*?"

"We *were* doing great," Seth muttered. He gave the salesclerk a sheepish smile before slinking off. "Buy the two-piece," he called.

The salesclerk shook her head. "I like that black tank, personally. It's very slimming."

Summer groaned. "Do you guys have a pay phone?"

The cell phone was ringing, but that didn't mean they had to pick it up, did it? Maria Marquez felt way too good, with the sun melting into her bones and the ocean lapping at her feet.

Next to her, Diana Olan stirred. "Are you deaf or what?"

"I've got sun-stun. Besides, it's your phone."

"I can't answer it. It might be my mother."

Marquez rolled onto her side. Fine white sand coated her Hawaiian Tropic-ed arm. She grimaced. "All right, chill, I'm coming," she muttered, digging through the canvas beach bag. She sat up, flipped open the phone, and collapsed with the effort. "Yeah?" she asked, adjusting her sunglasses.

"Marquez! Why are you answering Diana's phone? It's me, Summer! I'm at the Mall of America, and I need fashion help!"

"It's your cousin," Marquez reported to Diana. "She's having a mall crisis."

Diana lowered her shades. "Is she with Seth?"

"Is Seth with you?" Marquez asked Summer.

"He's at the food court. Eating fried cheese on a stick."

"Seth's having a fine-dining experience," Marquez said.

Diana nodded, apparently satisfied, and lay back on her towel.

"I haven't talked to you in ages," Marquez chided Summer. "What's up?"

"My parents got the last phone bill and freaked. Between you and Diana and Seth, I'm going to have to get a full-time job to pay for the long distance. I'm using up the last of my quarters on this call."

"Soon it won't be long distance," Marquez reminded her. "Guess where we are! This will get you psyched. We are lazing by the beach and it's eighty-one degrees and we've got my CD player cranked up on Hootie and the Blowfish and

5

there are four guys playing volleyball not fifty feet from here and they have *definitely* been hitting the Soloflex."

"It's thirty degrees here and sleeting. Why are you looking at other guys? Is everything okay with J.T.?"

"I guess." Marquez adjusted her bathing suit strap. "He's just a little, I don't know, distracted. Anyway, a girl can look, can't she?"

"Ask her how she and Seth are doing," Diana prompted.

Marquez shot her a dirty look. "I answered the phone, I ask the questions." She rolled onto her side. "So how are you and Sethie doing? Still drooling?"

"It's hard to do much drooling when he's in Wisconsin and I'm in Minnesota. He has to drive back this afternoon."

"Well, soon you two will have your own little love nest, courtesy of cousin Di. I saw a picture of the yacht," Marquez said. "I mean, this is some spring break hangout, Summer. Chandeliers and water beds and a big-screen TV. Oh, yeah, and a Jacuzzi in the shape of a heart, can you believe it?"

"This is going to be such a cool vacation." Summer sighed. "I miss you guys so much. I know I just saw you both at Christmas, but it seems like forever."

"We miss you, too. It's just way too weird, me

and Diana hanging out together solo. We need you around to keep us from trying to kill each other."

"I know what you mean," Summer said. Her voice was distant. "Diver and I have been going at it, too."

"Your sweet, innocent, incredibly gorgeous brother?" Marquez demanded. "I can't imagine Diver having a negative emotion. He's like . . . all Zen about everything."

"Not lately. Not like last summer." Summer sighed again. "I wish we were all back together. I wish everything was the way it was last summer, you know?"

"Yeah, I do. And it will be soon. Just a month or so."

"Six weeks, four days, and a few hours. But it's not like I'm obsessed or anything."

Marquez laughed. "So what's the fashion emergency?"

"Oh. I almost forgot. It's down to two choices. Two-piece, barely there, electric blue. Or black tank, fits really well, would be really good for swimming and jet-skiing and stuff."

"Summer, Summer, Summer. This is spring break, girl. In Florida, not Minne-so-dead. Definitely the two-piece."

"I can't wait to see you," Summer said softly. "I have to hang up now before the quarters run out, okay?"

"I'll call you next time."

"You're broke, too."

Marquez smirked at Diana. "Yeah, but Diana isn't."

Diana sat up and grabbed the phone. "Summer? I just wanted to say . . ." She turned away from Marquez, lowering her voice. "I just wanted to say I really miss you. . . . Yeah. Me too. . . . Yeah. Buy the two-piece, okay?"

She tossed the phone into her beach bag. Marquez stared at her, incredulous.

"What?" Diana demanded.

"'I really miss you'?" Marquez parroted. "Have you been out in the sun too long? If I didn't know you better, I'd swear that was like, you know, an actual emotion."

Diana almost looked hurt. "I like Summer a lot. I was a little hard on her last summer, but once I got to know her. . . . Anyway, she *is* my cousin."

Marquez eyed Diana suspiciously. "Still, you're being awfully nice to us, setting up this yacht and all. This isn't even your spring break. You graduated last year, remember?"

"But I kind of missed mine. So I'm compensating."

"You're compensating for *something*," Marquez said with a grin. "But I just can't figure out what."

"Oh, Maria," Diana said, knowing how much

Marquez hated being called by her first name. "Such a suspicious little mind. With the emphasis on *little*."

Marquez closed her eyes. The sun was like a sleeping potion. She'd figure out Diana another day, when she wasn't in a solar coma.

Next to her, Diana sighed. "She'll buy the tank, you know."

Marquez smiled fondly. "I know."

2

Good-byes Without Yawns and Good-byes Without Explanation

I miss you already," Seth whispered.

They were parked in his dilapidated Ford in front of Summer's home. He pulled her close—not an easy task, since they both had on down jackets—and lowered his lips to hers. It was a familiar kiss, warm and soft, and it occurred to her how comfortable she was with his safe, reliable, always-just-the-same kisses. How many times had he kissed her like this? Hundreds? Maybe even thousands?

To her horror, Summer suddenly felt a yawn coming. She tried to stifle it, forcing her mouth to stay closed, but it was no use. She yawned hugely. Her mouth opened to cavelike proportions.

Seth pulled away. "Sorry," he snapped. "Was I boring you?"

11

"You could never bore me," Summer said, placing her hand over his. "I'm just . . . I'm really sorry."

He ran his fingers through his thick chestnut hair. It was shorter than he'd worn it the previous summer, when they'd met, and his tan had faded to Wisconsin pale. But the great brown eyes hadn't changed—laughing and intense and thoughtful at the same time.

"*I* thought we were having a passionate kiss."

"We were. I didn't sleep very well last night, is all. My parents were fighting with Diver again." She made a little circle on the steamed-up window.

"So I wasn't putting you to sleep?"

"No! Was I putting *you* to sleep?"

"You're the one who yawned." After a moment Seth managed a lopsided grin. He patted her thigh. "Sorry. It'll be okay with Diver. He's just having a hard time right now."

"I guess."

Seth checked the stick-on clock on the peeling dashboard and sighed. "I need to get going."

"I feel like all we do is say good-bye to each other." Summer reached into the backseat to retrieve her shopping bags. "Wait, I almost forgot!" she exclaimed. "I bought you some stuff for the trip."

"So that's what took you so long. Cool. Presents!"

They weren't just presents, they were part of a scientifically designed plan to rekindle her romance with Seth. Summer knew about rekindling because she read her mother's *New Woman* magazine sometimes, and revving up a romance seemed to be a big concern for couples like her parents, not that she wanted to think about *that* too much. And since she and Seth were a long-term couple of nearly nine months (Summer insisted on counting from the day they'd met), she figured it might be time for a little rekindling.

Toward that end, she'd bought some of the items suggested in the article. Candles. A book called *101 Love Poems to Set the Mood*. A bottle of coconut-almond-papaya-scented suntan oil for rubbing on Seth's back while they basked in the Florida sun. And, from one of those Spencer kind of stores, a watch without hands. It was meant to symbolize that they weren't going to think about anything but each other. Seth was kind of obsessive about time.

Slowly Seth examined the items, one by one. He lingered on the tanning oil, grinning. When he got to the watch, he groaned.

"It's symbolic," Summer explained. "Five days without time pressures."

"You know, it's not like I'm obsessed," Seth said irritably. "Just because I know that when the big hand's on the twelve and the little hand's on the three it means it's three o'clock."

"I already said I was sorry at the mall," Summer snapped. "I lost track of time." They were doing it again. They always had nitpicky little fights right before saying good-bye.

Seth stroked her hair apologetically. "Thanks for all the cool stuff. Will you pack it for me? I'm just taking my backpack." He made a big ceremony of putting on the watch. Then he passed her a small paper sack from the backseat. "Here. For you, for the big trip. I went shopping, too."

She opened the bag. "Zinc oxide!" she said. It was precisely the same voice she used every Christmas when she opened one of her great-aunt's handmade sweaters.

"Green. For your nose, 'cause you know how you burn."

Summer smiled. "Thanks." It occurred to her that rekindling their romance might be more work than she'd thought.

She kissed Seth good-bye. In her mind, she was not in an uninspectable 1982 Ford with a hole in the floorboard. She was not wearing two pairs of thick wool socks in her Doc Martens. In her mind, she was already in Florida, touched by hibiscus-scented tropical breezes. The ocean was churning gently, waves breaking on a pristine white beach. The sun was kissing her bare shoulders with soothing heat.

This kiss, she didn't yawn once.

*   *   *

"Bought you something."

Summer tossed her Dayton's bag
her brother was lying on the couch in
room. *Oprah* was on. Diver's blue eyes
ted like a dozing cat's.

"It's a book," Summer said. She plopped
down onto the La-Z-Boy, her legs draped over
the arm. "*Guide to Southeastern Coastal Birds.*"

Diver brushed his blond hair out of his eyes. It
was darker than it had been the summer before.
The gold streaks from sun and salt water were
gone, and he'd cut it at their parents' insistence.
He studied the cover, which featured a pre-
historic-looking pelican. "Cool," he said vaguely.
"Thanks."

"It's for when we go down for spring break.
Aren't you getting excited about it? Going back
to Florida, I mean? It's been six months since
we've seen a palm tree, Diver. Or the ocean. Or a
big, fat, sunburned, hairy-backed tourist in a
Speedo."

Diver smiled wistfully. "Or a pelican. I miss
Frank."

"Me, too," Summer said, recalling the mega-
pooping pelican who'd resided on their porch.

"Sometimes it all seems so unreal," Diver said.
He looked at Summer with the clear, innocent
gaze that often made her feel as though he were
the younger sibling, even though he was two
years older. "Last summer, I mean, and finding

, and then coming here, and Jack and Kim, and . . . you know."

It still bothered Summer when he said that. Jack and Kim. Jack and Kim were Mom and Dad, his mom and dad, and hers. She didn't understand why Diver couldn't call them that, after all they'd suffered through. Why he couldn't say two little words.

Of course, her parents were no better. They called him Jonathan, when he was clearly Diver and always would be.

Summer grabbed the remote and switched to CNN. Diver didn't even blink. "I talked to Diana and Marquez today. Aunt Mallory has this friend with a yacht we can use."

Diver nodded noncommittally. He was thumbing through the bird book.

"Diver," Summer asked suddenly, "do you wish you'd stayed in Crab Claw Key? Do you hate it here in Minnesota?"

He smiled. It was pure smile, the kind of smile that she'd watched melt a hundred female hearts at Bloomington High School. "Well, it's very cold here," he said, as if that were an answer.

Their mother appeared in the doorway. Her coat was damp. She grimaced at Diver. "I thought you were working today."

"I called in sick." Lately Diver had been working as a stock boy at Target.

"Jonathan, this is just what happened with Burger King—"

Summer winced. She did not want to be around for this. "Mom, I got a great bathing suit," she interrupted. "Two, actually. Will you tell me what you think?"

Her mother hesitated, eyes flickering between Summer and Diver. "I've got a ton of groceries in the trunk," she said. "Come help." She pointed a finger at Diver. "We'll talk later."

Diver did not answer. He was tracing the pelican photo with his finger. "Frank had more brown here, around the eyes."

"I'll get the groceries," Summer said to her mother. "You check out my bathing suits. They're in the Dayton's bag. And try not to react like a mom, okay?"

Her mother gazed at Diver. "That's harder than you think," she said softly.

Summer lay in bed, her quilt tucked up around her chin. It was quiet. Finally.

There'd been another fight that evening. Slammed doors, loud voices. Mostly her parents' voices. Diver hardly ever argued. He just absorbed other people's words.

Sometimes she still had the dream. The one about the little boy chasing a red ball, about the day Diver had been lost to the family. Summer hadn't even been born yet, of course, so the

17

dream was just a collage of stories from her parents, from news clippings, and from Diver's own vague recollections. Not that he remembered much. He'd been kidnapped, he'd grown up knowing two other parents as his own, they'd been abusive, he'd run away.

Maybe he'd been on his own too long. Maybe that was why, when he and Summer had found each other by some crazy miracle the summer before, he hadn't seemed entirely sure about coming back to the family that was really his own. He was uncomfortable with rules and curfews and schoolwork. He didn't quite belong in Minnesota.

Summer slept fitfully. She kept hearing things: her door, a creak in the hallway, a sound from downstairs. She dreamed she was lying on a couch by the edge of the ocean, watching a pelican toss a little red ball in the air, then catch it in his great beak. Diver was there, too, but he was watching her. He said something, two words she could not quite make out, and then he dove into the water, swimming slowly away until he was just a speck on the horizon.

She woke up shivering beneath her quilt. Her pillow was wet with tears. It was a bleak, gray dawn. She sat up a little, quilt pulled close, and then she noticed the torn sheet of notebook paper on the edge of her bed.

She saw Diver's scrawl and the two words she had not been able to hear in her dream: *I'm sorry.*

And she knew he was really gone.

3

Spring Break, at Last— Let the Games Begin

*F*loss! Did I pack floss?" Summer sat in the airport terminal, carefully scanning her packing list.

"It's a little late now, you know," Seth said.

"I can't remember if I brought any socks."

"It's Florida. Socks are optional." Seth shook his head. "Are you listening to yourself? Even I'm not this anal."

Summer managed a smile. "It's just that I left in a hurry this morning, and my parents were fighting, and it was such a mess. . . . I just want everything to be perfect. No glitches."

"It will be. Guaranteed glitch-free."

"Ladies and gentlemen, we will now begin boarding passengers in rows one through twenty," a flight attendant announced.

Summer checked her ticket. "Not yet. I'm twenty-eight."

"Good. More time for kissing."

"We'll have plenty of time for that soon," Summer said, feeling a sudden rush of anticipation.

"Still, we should practice," Seth said. "It'll be two days before I see you again."

Summer kissed him again. "This is so crazy. I wish you were flying with me today. Couldn't your aunt have eloped?"

"She's my favorite aunt. I have to go to the wedding. Besides, my parents would kill me."

"Anyway, I'm glad you came to see me off."

"I thought you might need moral support, what with your mom and dad and all. . . ." Seth's voice dropped off.

"They actually said the word *separation* last night, Seth," Summer said. Tears filled her eyes as she recalled the angry shouts behind their bedroom door. "Ever since Diver left, it's like . . . like they can't even talk to each other. They blame each other for not handling it better." She gazed out the window at the big silver 727. "Me, I blame Diver."

"I'm not sure it's anybody's fault, Summer. It's just the way things are."

"You sound like Diver," she said accusingly. "Sometimes you have to work at stuff, Seth. He could have tried harder to fit in. And my parents could have tried harder to make him comfortable. I mean, look at you and me. We work at our relationship. It's hard being so far apart, but we work at it."

Seth toyed with a hole in the knee of her jeans. "I don't know. I don't exactly see it as *work*."

"You know what I mean. We're totally honest with each other. If Diver and my parents had just opened up more, told the truth about what they were feeling, things might have been different. I mean, I always know what you're feeling. And you always know what I'm feeling. That's how it's supposed to be. We'll never be like my parents."

Seth's gaze shifted for a moment. He opened his mouth to say something, then seemed to reconsider.

"What?"

"Nothing."

"Tell me."

Seth leaned close. She could smell the herbal shampoo he always used. He kissed her, long and hard, an all-out, backseat-of-the-car-on-a-date kiss. "There. That's all. That's all I wanted to tell you. I love you. We're not like your parents, okay?"

He almost sounded worried. "Okay," Summer said.

"Did you pack the candles and the suntan oil?"

21

"I may have forgotten the floss," Summer said, "but I remembered the important stuff."

From the bank of phones, Seth could see Summer's plane taxiing away. He felt the wrenching sadness that always overtook him when they had to separate. He ought to be used to it by now. They'd said plenty of good-byes, that was for sure.

He was so totally, completely, embarrassingly in love with Summer. He'd thought he'd been in love before, with a girl named Lianne, but that had just been his hormones talking. Not that his hormones weren't pretty much screaming with megaphones when he was with Summer. But this time it really was love. He loved the way she talked, the way she laughed, the way she kissed him . . .

And the way she trusted him. Summer was so good, so honest and straightforward. Not like him.

The memory came back again, unbidden. A snowy night over Christmas break. His car, stuck in a mountainous bank of fresh snow. The windows clouded with steam, the buzz of sneaked champagne, the feel of lips on skin. He felt a twinge of longing and then, instantly, a stab of horrible, aching regret.

He shook away the image. That was done and forgotten. Summer's life was complicated enough at the moment, and besides, he was not about to mess things up with her.

It was buried. Gone. No harm done.

Still, it wouldn't hurt to make sure it stayed that way.

He watched Summer's plane crawl slowly into the air. It took Seth a second to remember the Florida area code. His finger was shaking a little as he punched in the numbers, one by one.

Summer stared out the window, munching on her complimentary peanuts. She checked her watch. It had taken forever to get from Minneapolis to Orlando, but the last leg of the flight wouldn't take long. Already she could tell she was in Florida, even without stepping outside. The tarmac practically shimmered with heat. The sunshine was more intense, a brilliant yellow instead of a pallid pastel.

They'd had a forty-five-minute layover in Orlando, but soon the jet would be airborne again. A new line of passengers was boarding. She hoped no one had the seat in the middle. There was a nice, quiet woman on the end, and Summer had the window seat. From Minneapolis to Orlando they'd been stuck with a giant man who smelled like Ben-Gay and wouldn't stop jiggling his knees.

"Excuse me, that's me. Twenty-eight-B."

Summer looked up and nearly choked on a peanut.

An extremely amazing-looking guy was standing in the aisle. He tossed a dilapidated backpack on the floor by Summer's feet.

"Hi. I'm your seatmeat, uh, mate. Twenty-eight-B," Summer said, instantly feeling like plane dweeb of the century.

His dark eyes took her in without reaction. He worked to stuff a battered guitar case into the overhead compartment. Then, slipping gracefully past the woman on the aisle, he settled next to Summer.

She made it very clear she was busy staring out the window. Suddenly she wished she'd brought a book. She'd *meant* to—she was half-way through one of those romance series that never seem to end—but she'd been too frantic that morning to remember it. Of course, she had *101 Love Poems to Set the Mood,* but that hardly seemed like something she wanted to read in public.

She sneaked a glance at Twenty-eight-B. He was rifling through his backpack. He had a couple of tiny silver hoops in his ear and a shadow of beard. His dark hair did not seem to be operating under any kind of organizing principle. His jeans jacket was ripped and faded.

He reached for his seat belt and yanked on Summer's by mistake.

"Oh, is that you? Sorry."

"Mine's already fastened," Summer volunteered. She poked around near the armrest and located half of his belt. Unfortunately, it was directly underneath him. "Yours is . . . um, here. You're sitting on it," she said. She turned back to the window so he wouldn't see the blush creeping up her neck.

It was astonishing. Practically a whole year had passed since she'd gone to Florida to discover a new, more sophisticated, less aw-shucks-Midwestern-dork self. She'd had an actual real-live boyfriend for nine months already. You'd think she could talk to an attractive male without breaking into a cold sweat and stammering. Not to mention copping a feel.

She heard a click and knew he'd buckled up. The plane was starting to settle down. Stragglers were still trying to defy physics and stuff luggage into the overhead compartments. Flight attendants bustled back and forth, looking harried.

Twenty-eight-B pushed back his seat. Summer took another furtive glance while peanut-munching. His eyes were closed. He was holding a small spiral notebook with a pen clipped to it.

Suddenly he opened his eyes. His lids were rimmed in red. He was looking right at her.

"P-Peanut?" she managed, shoving the foil pack at him.

"Thanks."

He took the package from her and emptied

25

out a couple of peanuts. His fingers were trembling. Summer wondered if he was one of those people who were afraid to fly. What was that called, that plane phobia? She'd seen it on *Ricki Lake* once.

"Ladies and gentlemen, this is flight two-nineteen to Boca Beach, Florida," a flight attendant announced in a singsong voice. "We will be experiencing a slight delay in our scheduled departure time, but we do expect to be taking off shortly."

"Damn." Twenty-eight-B handed the peanuts back to Summer. "Let's get this show on the road, gang."

He sighed and rubbed his eyes with his hand. Oh, God, was he crying?

Summer tried to catch the attention of the woman seated on the aisle, but she was engrossed in *Glamour*. They should do something, shouldn't they? Calm him before the flight started or something. What if he freaked when they were airborne? Threw open the emergency door so they'd all be sucked into oblivion?

She could at least make small talk. Distract him.

"The last time I flew down to Florida," Summer said brightly, "I sat next to this woman with tarot cards—you know, they're supposed to tell the future?—and she told me I was going to meet three guys that summer, one mysterious, one dangerous, and one the right one"—oh, no,

26

her mouth was taking the express route now, but there was no stopping it—"and it's not like I believe you can see the future or anything, but the weird thing is, I really did meet three guys, and they really were what she'd said, and . . ."

She ran out of gas. The guy was staring at her blankly. Well, not entirely blankly. There was this half-smile on the right side of his very nice lips, as if that was all the energy he had to commit to the effort.

"You'll be pleased to hear I'll be shutting up now," she said lamely. "I know I was rambling. I was just trying to take your mind off . . . whatever."

"Were you sorry?" he asked softly. "About that lady with the tarot cards? Knowing what was going to happen?"

"Well, it wasn't like I really believed her. So it was just sort of funny when she turned out to be right."

"But what if you *had* believed her?" He asked it as if the answer really mattered.

Summer thought. "I couldn't have. I mean, I'm just not into that stuff. I don't even read my horoscope, except on my birthday."

Twenty-eight-B checked his watch. "This is a bad idea," he murmured. "You know how sometimes you just know in your gut?"

"What's a bad idea? Flying, you mean?"

He stared past her out the window.

27

"You're not like . . . having a premonition, are you? Of us crashing or something?" Summer inquired. She didn't believe in premonitions either. Still, it wouldn't hurt to hear him out.

"I can't do this."

She looked at him and saw such sadness in his dark eyes that for a brief, insane moment she wanted to reach out and hold him.

He flipped open his seat belt, grabbed his backpack, and practically hurdled over the *Glamour* woman. He retrieved his guitar and sprinted down the aisle, brushing past a flight attendant. After he vanished into the first-class section, Summer could hear a loud exchange of voices.

"What's with him?" the *Glamour* woman asked.

"I think maybe he had a premonition."

"Yeah, I get those every time I fly. Course, nothing ever comes of them. Knock wood."

The loud voices stopped. Summer peeked over the seat in front of her. She couldn't see anything. Twenty-eight-B had vanished.

She noticed his notebook on the floor and picked it up. Should she go after him? What if it was important? Maybe there was an address inside. When she got to Boca Beach, she could mail it to him.

Feeling a little guilty, she opened to the first page. No address. Just *Works in Progress.* Summer randomly flipped through the pages.

A title caught her eye. *Sonnet to a Girl Unmet.*

Oh, well. One line wouldn't hurt: *That I have not yet met your gentle gaze.*

Quickly Summer moved on. There was something too personal about what she was doing. It was like rummaging through someone's underwear drawer. She saw other poems, musical notes, long passages with tight writing. But she couldn't find an address.

Summer motioned to a flight attendant hurrying past. "The guy who was sitting here, Twenty-eight-B? Is he gone?"

"We explained we're just about to take off." She rolled her eyes, adjusting the crisp silk bow tie at her collar.

"So he's gone."

"Yes," the woman said impatiently. "Did you need something?"

"He left this—" Summer started to hand her the tattered notebook. Suddenly she remembered the desperate look in his eyes. She could not just give *Sonnet to a Girl Unmet* to this indifferent flight attendant. She could picture the little notebook in a lost-and-found at the terminal, could see the sweaty guys from maintenance laughing at the contents.

"Miss, I'm sort of in a hurry here."

"I . . . never mind," Summer said.

She watched the flight attendant hustle away. She flipped through the rest of the notebook. On the final page was a scrawled note. *Testing Thursday, March 21, 2 P.M., Dr. Mitchell, outpatient clinic.*

Summer stared at the words. A doctor's appointment, that Thursday. Testing. That did not sound good.

She grabbed her purse and pushed past the *Glamour* lady. "Next time I'm getting the window seat," the woman muttered.

Summer ran down the aisle, notebook clutched in her hand. At the exit, another flight attendant, this one a middle-aged man, was waiting.

"You're making a big mistake," the flight attendant warned, but Summer was already running out the door, and she already had a pretty good idea what kind of mistake she was making.

4

Missed Flights and Missing Friends

Summer stopped by a check-in counter, panting, and scanned the area. No sign of Twenty-eight-B.

"Ladies and gentlemen, this is the final boarding call for flight two-nineteen to Boca Beach, Florida."

Her heart was pounding like a jackhammer. This was crazy. She didn't even know this guy. She was risking her spring break for a complete stranger, even if he was a complete stranger with the most penetrating, sad, tearful eyes she'd ever seen. So what if he wrote sonnets? He could be an ax murderer. A poetic ax murderer who wore uncomfortable contacts.

As she started to retreat, a flash of dark hair and a jean jacket caught her eye.

Him. Definitely him.

"Hey!" she called, causing numerous travelers to stop and turn. "Twenty-eight-B!" But he had already disappeared into a rest room.

She ran to the entrance of the men's room. A young guy about her age was heading in.

Summer grabbed his arm. "Would you mind taking this in there for me?" she asked breathlessly. "There's a guy with a guitar. Kind of broody looking, with really pretty eyes."

He scowled at the notebook, then grinned at her. "What is this, a drug pass or something?"

"No, it's just love poems. Look, I'm going to miss my plane. Tell him it's from Twenty-eight-B."

The guy pulled from her grasp. "You want me to, like, go into a men's room and hand some guy a bunch of love poetry? I look like I have a death wish?"

The guy moved on. Summer swallowed. Already the plane was probably pulling away, leaving her behind to spend her all-time-perfect senior-year romance-rekindling spring break stuck outside a men's room in Orlando.

No way. She had too much at stake.

Covering her eyes, Summer pushed open the men's room door. "Twenty-eight-B, you left your notebook," she yelled. She pulled back her arm and tossed with all her might. "Bye. Have a nice life."

Bye? Have a nice life? Summer groaned as she

dashed out the door. Good thing she was never going to see him again.

If she ran, really ran, she might still make the plane.

"Wait. Wait up!"

Summer stopped abruptly. It was him. He had this deep, soft, unforgettable kind of voice to go with the unforgettable eyes. A matched set. She turned.

He was standing by the men's room door. He held the notebook by one corner between his fingers. It was dripping wet.

"I know it's not Shakespeare," he said. "But really, right into the toilet? Talk about a tough critic."

"I didn't—I mean, it was great poetry, not that I really read any, but . . . I-I have to go," Summer stammered. "The plane, I'm on spring break—"

He pointed to a long row of windows. A big 727 was pulling away, moving in slow motion like a sleek dinosaur.

Her 727.

Summer slumped against the wall. "I can't believe it," she whispered. "I am such a jerk."

Twenty-eight-B leaned against the wall with her. He shook the notebook. It dribbled on the dirty gray carpet. "What if I turn out to be the next Shakespeare? You'll have done the world a great service."

Summer stared at him, bereft. "It's my spring break."

"I'm really sorry, Twenty-eight-B."

She sighed. "Summer."

"That's the spirit. To hell with spring break. There's always summer vacation."

"No. That's my name. Summer. Like the season, with a capital."

He digested this information. "I'm Austin. Like the capital, with a capital."

They sat there in silence. Summer considered crying, but she was too annoyed at herself to cry.

"I'm really sorry about this," Austin said.

"Why did you jump off the plane, anyway?" Summer demanded, suddenly feeling angry with him for no particular reason other than the fact that she needed somebody to be angry at. "Are you afraid to fly?"

"Depends on the destination." Austin sounded almost cheerful now, which Summer found especially annoying. He nodded toward the main terminal. "Come on. I'll buy you a cappuccino. It's the least I can do."

Summer shook her head.

"Latte? Mocha java?"

Summer shook her head again. What should she do next? Call Diana, for a start. If she didn't catch Diana and Marquez before they headed for Boca Beach, they'd be stuck waiting for her. And she needed to get to a ticket agent and find out when the next available flight left. Maybe it would only be an hour or two.

"Double espresso? Double foamless no-fat latte with amaretto?"

Summer smiled, just a little. He looked so cute, standing there with his wet poetry. And it wasn't as if she was in a hurry, not anymore. "How about a plain coffee?" she said.

Austin grinned. "After all you've been through on my behalf, I might even throw in a jelly doughnut."

Summer slid into the coffee shop booth, where Austin was on his second cup of coffee. "We can't get on another flight until eight-forty tonight," she reported.

"Did you explain to the ticket agent that you missed your flight because you were rescuing timeless art?"

"I told her you were one of those plane phobics. She said they get a couple of plane jumpers every week." Summer shrugged. "At least the plane wasn't airborne."

He laughed. "Did you get hold of your friend?"

"No. I tried Diana and Marquez. No luck."

Austin grinned. He held out a salt shaker like a microphone. "Summer Smith, you've just missed your flight connection!" he said in an announcer's boom. "Now where are you going?"

She looked at him blankly. "To sit in an uncomfortable chair for a few hours?"

"Wrong!" Austin boomed. "You're going to Walt Disney World!"

Summer sipped her coffee. "I don't think so."

"Come on," Austin urged. "It'll be a hoot."

"A hoot?"

"A lark, a gas, a riot, a diversion, a romp . . . that's the best I can do. My thesaurus is in my backpack." He tilted his head a little. He had a very nice smile. Very nice. "Come on. I checked while you were on the phone. We can take one of the express hotel buses right to Mickeyland. We'll spend a few hours, get back in plenty of time for you to catch your plane—"

"*My* plane? What about you?"

"A mere slip of the tongue, my girl. *Our* plane," Austin said lightly. He leaned across the table. The growth of beard made his eyes seem even darker. "Have you ever been?"

"I went to Disneyland in California when I was four."

The truth was, she didn't remember much about it. She'd been devastated when she lost her mouse ears during the teacup ride. The previous summer she and Seth had talked about taking a road trip from Crab Claw Key up to Disney World. They'd just never been able to work out the timing.

Summer sighed. "Anyway, it's too expensive. Besides, I hardly know you."

"I'm buying. I owe you. After all, you saved my notebook. And as for knowing me, what are you worried about? This is like the ultimate chaperoned date. There are thousands of Mousenoids scurrying about, keeping the dazed tourists in line. What could possibly go wrong?"

Summer hesitated. It would be crazy to go. The logical thing would be to stay in the airport, watch CNN on one of the lounge TVs, and eat candy bars.

Of course, she was officially on spring break. And you were allowed to be a little crazy during spring break.

Instantly a tiny, annoying voice in her head began chanting, What about Seth? What about Seth?

"I have a boyfriend," she blurted suddenly.

"I'm not at all surprised," Austin replied.

"I mean, just so you know."

"Look," Austin said, "you can hang around here for the next few hours, dozing off and drooling on your neighbor, or you can visit the Magic Kingdom with me. It's the happiest place on earth, you know."

"I don't drool."

"Point taken."

Summer thought. Austin, meanwhile, began softly singing, "It's a small world after all, it's a small world after all . . ."

"If I go, will you stop singing that?" Summer asked.

"It's from one of my favorite rides, with these Children of the Damned animatronic puppets. At the end of the ride a tiny microchip with the lyrics is surgically implanted in your brain."

Summer laughed. "I really need to call my cousin and let her know about the plane," she said, stalling.

"I'm taking a big leap here, but I'll lay even money they have phones at Disney World."

Summer fiddled with the napkin in her lap. Seth never had been very psyched to go to Disney World. This might be her one big chance.

Still, she wasn't sure what to say.

"Come on," Austin whispered in that soft, sexy voice. "I'll even buy you mouse ears."

And then, suddenly and quite certainly, Summer knew the answer.

The car phone was ringing, and Diana was still searching through her purse for her keys. At last she found them, struggled with the lock, and threw open the door to her Neon. "Figures," she muttered when she was rewarded with a dial tone. She was not having good luck with phones. She'd already had one very disturbing long-distance call that day.

She hoped it was Marquez. Marquez was supposed to have met her there an hour earlier. Now they were going to get to Boca Beach late and would probably miss Summer's arrival. And poor

Summer would undoubtedly panic and start calling every cop in Florida.

Diana revved the engine. Well, maybe that was a tiny bit unfair. Sweet, wholesome, maximum-Midwestern Summer had acquitted herself pretty well the previous summer, when she'd come to stay in Crab Claw Key. Truth was, Diana was actually looking forward to seeing her cousin. It had been a long time, punctuated with the occasional postcard or call. Of course, there had been the big, heartwarming Christmas-vacation family hugathon in the frigid north, but it hadn't turned out all that well. Not that there was any point in dwelling on *that*.

Diana drove down the palm-studded narrow road that held together the islands off the tip of Florida like beads on a string. It was an intensely sunny, cloudless day, and the turquoise ocean was alive with light. She passed two guys on bright yellow windsurfers and waved.

Diana lowered her window. It was hot for March, nearly eighty-five degrees, and she was glad she'd worn a tube top and white cotton shorts. Her suitcases—all three of them—were in the trunk. She hoped Marquez had packed light. She hoped Marquez had packed, period.

Marquez lived near the center of the little town in a converted store. It was a far cry from Diana's house, a fanciful and overwrought near-mansion in pastel colors that befit its owner.

After all, Mallory Olan, Diana's mother, *was* a best-selling romance novelist.

Marquez's family, on the other hand, had been in some financial trouble lately, from what Diana understood. Not that Marquez would talk about it much, but the For Sale sign on the front lawn told the story.

Diana parked and leaned on the horn a couple of times. No response. She blared the horn again.

"Hey, lighten up," came a familiar male voice.

J.T., Marquez's boyfriend—*former* boyfriend—poked his head in the open window. He was cute, in that scruffy way that appealed to someone like Marquez. Too bad he was a jerk.

"You seen Marquez anywhere?"

"Why would you be looking for her, slime puppy?"

J.T. looked pained. "It wasn't working, you know?"

"*It.* Would that be a portion of your anatomy that shall remain nameless?"

"It works fine, thank you very much. I just mean, you know, she was getting all clingy."

"Boy-code for 'I need fresh meat.'"

J.T. rolled his eyes. "Look, she didn't show up for her lunch shift at work. I called and the phone was always busy, so I came over to check it out. Does that sound like the act of a slime puppy?"

Diana stepped out into the blinding sun. "I am definitely not getting involved, J.T. Come on, let's find the girl. We're supposed to pick up Summer in Boca Beach. Besides, Marquez and I went shopping last night, and she walked off with my gold card. She's on my most-wanted list."

J.T. shook his head, laughing. "Walked off, as in stole?"

"Walked off, as in 'I always wanted to hold one of these suckers, Diana, do you mind?' An honest mistake."

"Uh-huh." J.T. pounded on the front door, then pulled a key out of his pocket.

"You dumped her and kept her key?"

J.T. shrugged. He slipped the key in the lock.

The entryway was cool and dark. Marquez's bedroom was to the right, in what had been an old-fashioned ice cream parlor in another life. It was, Diana had to admit, a very cool room, and she felt a sudden pang for Marquez as they stepped into it. She must be bummed her family was selling the place, and to have it topped off by losing J.T. . . . well, his timing sucked.

The room was total chaos, as usual. Clothes hanging from lamps. An open package of Oreos on the bed. Art materials—paints and brushes and sketch pads and pastels—scattered here and there. Marquez was a fantastic artist, although she persisted in believing she was going to be a fantastic lawyer someday. That was about as likely as Diana becoming a fantastic Sunday school teacher.

J.T. looked melancholy. "I kinda miss her already."

"Shoulda thought of that, I guess."

Diana's gaze fell on the main focus of Marquez's room, a giant mural that Marquez added to whenever she was in the mood. Fabulous palm trees climbed up to the ceiling, and faces and names covered the wall in Day-Glo colors. It was so Marquez, so out there, so in-your-face. Diana could never look at it without feeling both amazed and a little embarrassed.

But something had changed since the last time she'd seen the mural. In the corner, scrawled in big, careless, loopy letters, was a simple message: *I am outa here.*

J.T. was looking at it, too. "I'll go check upstairs," he said grimly. "You check for clues."

"Clues?"

"She's run off. She's gone. That piece-of-crap car of hers is gone, she ripped off your credit card, and there's that note. What do you think's going on, Sherlock?"

While J.T. went upstairs, Diana scanned the room. Who knew what to look for? Marquez's room was as disorderly as her life. Had Marquez been depressed the night before? She'd shrugged off the J.T. breakup, talked a little about her parents selling the house. And she was mad about not getting into the Ivy League colleges she'd applied to.

Still, it wasn't Diana's fault she hadn't noticed Marquez was truly upset. Marquez wasn't easy to read. She was always so up, so flip about everything, or else she was totally enraged. She had the emotional depth of a Doberman puppy.

J.T. appeared in the doorway. "One of her brothers was up there, crashed on the couch. He's working a night shift, so he had the phone off the hook. He said Marquez split this morning. She left her parents a note saying she'd get in touch soon."

Diana sighed. "I wouldn't even know where to start looking for her."

"You know Marquez. She'll find you when she's good and ready."

Outside, the thick, oppressive heat came as a surprise. A family wearing matching T-shirts Rollerbladed by awkwardly.

"I guess she didn't tell you," J.T. said suddenly.

"Tell me?"

"She found me yesterday. With this waitress, this new girl. In my apartment."

"Ah. The plot thickens. And were you, as they say, in a state of undress?"

J.T. grimaced. "Coulda been."

"Actually, she didn't tell me. She just said you two broke up and that it was about time." Diana shook her head. "You pig."

"I'm not a pig. It was just . . . you know, it just kind of happened. You know?"

Diana examined a thumbnail. "Yeah, I know. Stuff happens sometimes. That doesn't mean you're not a scumbag, J.T. It just means . . . well, lots of people are scumbags. Lots of people."

5

Magic Kingdom, Magic Kissing

"Come on. Hug Goofy. Give him a big, wet kiss."

Summer conceded a brief handshake with the big costumed Disney employee.

"Now smile and say kibble," Austin instructed. He clicked the little disposable camera he'd bought at the gift shop near the entrance to Disney World.

"You must be really hot in there," Summer said to Goofy.

Goofy pantomimed wiping his brow with a big, gold, velvet dog paw.

Austin ran over to join them. "Nice work, boy," he said. "What do they pay you, anyway? I always kind of wanted to work at Disney before I die. It's sort of like joining the military, only with better uniforms."

He led Summer down a turn-of-the-century thoroughfare called Main Street USA. Ice cream parlors, shops, and cafés lined the street, all picture-perfect re-creations. The area was crowded with parents and kids. Many of the children were clutching silver helium balloons in the shape of mouse ears. Some kids looked dazed and a little overwhelmed, which was how Summer was feeling. Some looked as though they'd landed in heaven, which was how Austin was looking. It amazed her how his demeanor had shifted from sensitive, tortured poet on the plane to happy-go-lucky kid at Disney World.

He paused to snap a picture of Snow White in front of a pink-and-yellow gingerbread cottage. "Show me a little leg, Snow," he urged, but she just waved demurely.

"Why are you taking so many pictures?" Summer asked.

"We're having Kodak moments here, Summer," Austin replied. "I'm preserving this so you can remember me when I'm gone."

"Are you planning on going somewhere?" Summer asked as she swerved to avoid two little girls dressed in identical King Kong T-shirts.

"They've been to Universal Studios," Austin said. "Too bad we don't have more time. They have some excellent rides."

"You didn't answer my question."

"About going somewhere? No, I don't have

46

any plans. I have less than no plans, as it happens." His expression changed for a moment. Then he was all smiles again. "What's that saying? 'Man plans, God laughs'?" He reached for Summer's arm. "Speaking of tomorrow, how about we start there?"

"Where?"

"Tomorrowland. They've got a great roller coaster, Space Mountain. We'll head over to Fantasyland and take the Skyway over. See those chairlift-type things going over the park? Game?"

"Sure. Whatever you want. As long as I get those mouse ears. But . . . are you sure? What about your fear of heights?"

"I'm not afraid of heights."

"Of airplanes, then."

Austin stopped, hands on hips. "Summer, my dear, you're really not getting into the spirit of this place. This is the Magic Kingdom. We are in a problem-free zone. Mickey is a mellow, Prozac kind of guy, okay?"

She smiled. There was something awfully charming about Austin. She thought instantly of Seth and had a major guilt spasm.

She told herself to lighten up. There was nothing wrong with noticing that she was with a majorly attractive guy with broad shoulders and brooding eyes who wrote sonnets to girls unmet. It didn't mean anything. And after all, she *was* on spring break.

"I can tell you're still thinking." Austin's voice was accusatory. "That's a felony in Disney World. Go Zen. Live in the moment, okay?"

"Okay," Summer said. "The moment. Gotcha."

"So why are you frowning?" Austin asked, leading her down a path lined with bright red flowers. They seemed especially exotic in March, with Minnesota still swathed in snow.

"You said Zen. That made me think of my brother. He's kind of like the ultimate in mellow. I mean, he was."

"He's—"

"Oh, no, he's alive. I mean, I *hope* he is. He left home a month and a half ago because he couldn't hack this stuff with my parents and . . . well, it's a long story."

"That would qualify as a non-Disneyesque anecdote," Austin said. "No backgrounds, no life stories, no yearbook pictures. We're suspended in time. We have no past and no future."

Soon they were in line for the Skyway. Austin busied himself studying the Disney World map with great intensity. It occurred to Summer that she knew virtually nothing about her escort for the afternoon.

"You know, you could at least tell me some basic stuff," she said. "Like where you're from. Where you're going. Your last name. Stuff."

Austin rolled his eyes. "Missouri, Boca Beach, Reed. Satisfied?"

"Minnesota, Boca Beach, Smith."

"So it seems we have at least one thing in common."

"Are you in college?" Summer asked. She couldn't help being a little curious.

"University of Texas, freshman, dropped out after a semester." Austin crossed his arms, daring her to ask any more.

"I guess you don't want me to ask why."

"You are nothing," he said with a smile, "if not perceptive."

Summer watched a group of children load onto one of the Skyway trams, a large bucketlike cable car open to the air on all sides. "I read this book once," she said, to change the subject. "This guy and girl were trapped on the Skyway when it broke down, and she was afraid of heights, and he kissed her to calm her down."

Way to keep the conversation going, Summer. Could you sound a little more pathetically desperate?

Austin rubbed his chin thoughtfully. "So this was one of Hemingway's later works?"

She laughed. "I guess you're really into books and stuff, huh?"

"I like to read, yeah. I often prefer the fictional world to the real one. You don't like the ending, you toss out the book and try another."

"You write poetry, too. That's cool."

The line inched forward. "How much did you

read?" Austin asked, head cocked. "In my note-book?"

"None. Well, a little. Hardly any."

"I feel so . . . so naked, so exposed, so . . ." Austin fanned his face. "Sorry, I was getting excited there for a minute." He grinned, clearly enjoying the blush that crept up Summer's neck.

"I'm sorry. It's like reading someone's diary or something, isn't it? I was just looking for an address so I could mail your notebook to you."

Suddenly she remembered the clinic appointment. A question formed in her mind, but she knew it would be a mistake to ask Austin. That really was getting too personal.

"Anyway," she said, "I liked the one about the unmet girl. The tiny bit I read."

Austin was watching her with a mysterious half-smile. "Maybe I'll change it to *met* girl," he said softly.

"And over there's Cinderella's Golden Carousel, and down there, see the turquoise water? That's Captain Nemo's ship, from *Twenty Thousand Leagues Under the Sea.*"

Austin sat beside her, his arm draped loosely over Summer's shoulders. He made a very enthusiastic tour guide.

"How many times have you been here, Austin?"

"Quite a few. Enough to know all the words to the *Pirates of the Caribbean* song. 'Yo-ho, yo-ho—'"

"I get the idea. When's the last time you came here?"

He paused. His eyes flickered, as if they'd lost their place in a text. "With my dad and my brother. Three, four years ago."

"What's your dad do?" She couldn't seem to stop herself from asking questions. He was being so mysterious.

Austin blinked. The happy face returned. "Wrong. Deduct ten points. That would qualify as being outside Disney parameters. But that's okay. You're a Disney virgin." He gave her that silly, suggestive grin. "Of course, we could change that if you like."

Summer laughed. It was a come-on line. At least, uttered by one of the guys at school with a suggestive leer, it would have been. But coming from Austin, even with his dark, older looks, it seemed charming and almost innocent.

"For the record," Austin said, gazing down at the pastel world below, "my dad's a cellist. Was, I guess I should say."

Summer could tell by his tone of voice that the subject was closed. For a while they sat in silence. The Skyway car moved slowly, floating through the air like a huge egg.

Austin gazed at her thoughtfully. "By the way, you're not afraid of heights, are you?"

"Me? No, why? You're the one who jumped off the plane."

"I was thinking about that book you told me about. Hoping maybe life could imitate art."

Again the flirtation, but it didn't quite seem sincere. They were just words, the right words he felt he had to say. He was thinking of something else. Someone else, maybe. Summer couldn't get over the odd feeling that he was trying hard to be upbeat but that something was bothering him, something big.

"You know," she said, "I'm really glad I came. You were right. This is a lot more fun than hanging out at the airport."

Austin patted her hand. "Thanks for coming. It would have been a drag being here alone." He winked. "After this, mouse ears, I promise."

The car stopped suddenly.

"You don't think we've broken down, do you?" Summer asked.

"It would certainly be a stroke of irony," Austin said. "That is, if life was imitating art, of course."

"But it isn't."

"No. Not likely."

Summer could feel him looking at her. She could feel the slight press of his hard shoulder against hers. A completely innocent touch, warm, just a grazing, really. But it sent shock waves all the way down her arm.

"So why are we just hanging here?" she asked, her voice squeakier than was strictly necessary.

"It happens. I got caught in the Jungle Ride once for an hour and a half. Disney World, like life, isn't perfect."

"In that book the girl was all freaked out, of course."

"While you, on the other hand, are the picture of calm."

"You know, I have a boyfriend," Summer said again, for no particular reason. I have a boyfriend who is sweet and wonderful and loves me to death, and besides, I'm spending spring break with him, so what am I doing, pressing my thigh just the tiniest bit closer to yours?

He was still looking at her when she finally met his eyes. "You have a boyfriend," he said very quietly. He was smiling, but only a little now. A wistful, sad, many-miles-away kind of smile.

"His name is Seth," Summer whispered, and then Austin touched her cheek and he was kissing her, soft and slow, and she didn't even notice when the ride started up again.

"Sometimes," Austin murmured as their lips parted gently, "life is better than fiction."

6

Accidents Will Happen, Even to Big, Ugly Birds

Marquez was doing eighty, and it felt good. Eighty-five felt even better.

Her battered Honda was rattling like a leaf in a tropical storm, but Marquez didn't care. She was in the eye, she was in the calm center, she was at the controls of Hurricane Marquez.

With the windows down, she could barely hear the Ramones pouring out of the portable cassette player on the floor. But that didn't matter—she was dancing anyway. With her right foot jerking out the beat on the accelerator, the car surged and fell back, eliciting stares as she passed the more law-abiding cars in the right lane.

She was moving. She was going nowhere, but she was moving. And when she was moving, she didn't have to think. Not about J.T., not about school, not about the house. . . . It was so easy. That morning, after she'd left, she'd spent a while just moping on the beach, licking her wounds, unsure what to do next. Then, suddenly, in a burst of inspiration, it had come to her. It was the ultimate answer to her problems: Leave them. Geo-therapy.

The land rolled past, flat and swampy, one mile indistinguishable from the next. She had no particular goal in mind, except that she knew she'd have to stop and pee soon. Sleep, too, although she was so buzzed on diet Coke she figured she could drive straight to Canada, assuming her bladder held out.

She'd left in style, at least. Just a simple note, nothing more, on her wall. And she'd been cool enough to leave a note for her parents, too. No point in freaking them out.

It would have been nice to call Diana, probably, but Diana would have had all these logical objections to register. Such as, Go, girl, but leave my gold card behind.

The only one Marquez felt really bad about was Summer. She hated to put a damper on Summer's big spring break plans. When Marquez had driven past the exit for Boca Beach a while back, she'd had a twinge of regret, but she had to put her own needs first. And they boiled down to one thing, pretty much: no thinking, no way.

Summer liked to think. Marquez had almost

called her the night before, but Summer would have had all these nice, sweet things to say, such as, There are other fish in the sea. Yeah, that was a Summery kind of thing to say, and she would have meant it, too, and she might even have been right.

Summer didn't get seriously, all-out angry. She didn't understand what it was like to be high on a rage, the way Marquez was right then, all engines on full throttle.

Diana did. Diana was capable of forming a serious hate. When a senator's son had assaulted her, she'd found a way to exact revenge. It had required time and patience and even a bit of blackmail, but then, that was Diana's style. Marquez had to admire that about the girl.

Marquez was not the patient type, however. She had feelings, she went with them. And that day they were taking her on a trip up the coast of Florida to who knew where.

As soon as she found a place to pee.

"Crescent Island, population six hundred and fifty," Marquez read as she slowed the Honda to a crawl a half-hour later. Without the wind, the Ramones were almost too loud. Almost.

"The question is, does a town of six hundred and fifty warrant a McDonald's?" Marquez muttered. She was starting to feel just the tiniest bit down. The caffeine was losing its edge. Her thighs were plastered to the hot vinyl seat. She felt as though she needed a stingingly cold shower.

She took an access road. Ahead was an ancient drawbridge spanning a thin expanse of blue-green water. On the far side was Crescent Island. Marquez could make out a handful of bobbing, aging boats and a couple of dilapidated bait shops. No McDonald's, nothing even post-fifties. Bad choice. She should have stayed on the interstate.

At the edge of the bridge, traffic, such as it was, slowed as a barrier with a flashing red light on it came down. "Fantastic," Marquez muttered. She put the car in neutral. Her knee would not stop jumping. She felt uneasy in her own skin.

Overhead, pelicans soared back and forth along the bridge, taking advantage of the wind currents. Ugly birds. Bridge pigeons. Diver and Summer had had a pelican living with them on their stilt house the past summer. What had Diver called it? Phil? He'd actually claimed to be able to talk to the bird, but then that was Diver all over. Who knew? Maybe he really could. Marquez had attempted a flirtation with Diver, but she'd never been able to get through to him. Well, maybe she shouldn't feel so bad. Obviously Summer and her family hadn't gotten through to Diver either.

It suddenly occurred to her that Diver had

more or less rejected her, and now J.T. had most definitely rejected her, and maybe that meant something. . . . Stop thinking. She cranked up the volume. "The only thing to live for is today," she sang. The boys had that much right.

An anemic little sailboat chugged past, and the drawbridge slowly closed. Marquez revved the engine and took off toward the island. On the far side of the bridge she scanned the town for a sign of a toilet that wouldn't make her skin crawl.

Nothing. She might as well turn around, hit the highway, and hope for a Denny's or something. She kept driving, aimlessly searching for a convenient place to turn around, and before she knew it the town had evaporated and she was on an isolated two-lane road about a hundred feet from the water's edge.

It was pretty in a desolate sort of way. Marquez gazed off at the water. Suddenly a flash of white coming from the right caught her eye, and then there was a terrible, soft thud.

A bird. She'd hit a bird. She glanced in her rearview mirror. A damn pelican. It figured. As if she needed this now.

She pulled to the side of the road. It was flopping around in the sea grass like a demented dancer. She waited, hoping some animal good Samaritan would happen along. Could she just drive off? Was it a hit-and-run when the victim was a big, ugly bird?

The pelican stopped moving. That really sucked, because it meant she was going to have to think, and once she started she might never stop.

Marquez walked back to the bird. It looked up at her with a beady, accusatory eye. "Hey, it was an accident," Marquez muttered. "I had the right of way."

It flapped one wing. She was pretty sure the wing was not supposed to be hanging at such an odd angle.

"What am I supposed to do now?" Marquez wailed out loud. She suddenly felt very sorry for herself, which just made her feel worse, since she knew she should be feeling sorry for the poor broken pelican.

There was a tiny gas station half a mile up the road. "Stay here," Marquez instructed, but it seemed pretty clear the pelican wasn't going anywhere. Was the bird breathing a little funny? Did pelicans breathe? Of course they did. She wasn't thinking clearly. She wasn't tracking.

The clerk at the gas station was old and wiry and drinking a Fresca. Her leathery skin hung in folds. Marquez made a mental note to use more sunscreen.

"I hit this pelican," Marquez confessed.

"Happens all the time."

"Do you have a bathroom I could use?"

"No bathroom for tourists."

"But I'm not a tourist. I live here. I live in Florida, I mean. And I'm sort of an accident victim, technically."

The woman pushed a rotary phone across the counter. "Call pelicans."

"I know they're called pelicans. What do I do about it? Is there a vet or something around here?"

"555-8121. Peli-*Ken's*. He'll know."

Marquez dialed the number. Maybe Ken would have a bathroom. "Is he, like, a bird sanctuary or something?"

"Peli-Ken's," came a raspy voice before the woman could answer. "State your bird emergency."

"I . . . I hit one. A pelican. It was an accident, I—"

"Location?"

Marquez handed the phone to the woman, who explained where they were, then passed the phone back to Marquez.

"Do not attempt to handle the bird."

"Don't worry, I won't."

"But try to keep it calm."

"How?" Marquez demanded, but the line was already buzzing.

She headed back to the injured bird. It looked calm enough to be dead, except for that angry eye it kept blinking at her. She sat in the tall grass and waited for someone to come.

She'd drawn a pelican once, on her mural.

God, that was a good mural, and now it would be lost forever. Somebody new would buy her house and paint over it in some awful pastel. It was like knowing someone was going to die. Well, in a way someone was. All the old parts of her—her dreams, her boyfriend, her home—were disappearing before her eyes.

A van was approaching. It had a painting of a pelican on the side—Marquez could have done a much better job—and tires so bald they were shiny. A blond guy was driving. Even from this distance she could see he was probably very good-looking. Strange, since on the phone Ken had sounded like an old geezer.

Marquez rocked back and forth. She was getting very tired. The stress of smushing a bird and all that. She wished she knew where she was going. A destination wouldn't be such a bad thing.

She was coming down from the high of leaving, she told herself. But she knew it was something else. She knew that by nightfall she'd be right back where she'd been the night before—cursing J.T. and sobbing his name, tangled up in hot sheets.

She wished she had a bathroom.

She wished she knew where the hell she was going.

The van stopped. The windshield was dusty. The door opened.

Marquez looked at the bird. "Here comes your savior."

"Marquez?"

Marquez looked back at the van. She blinked. She looked again.

"Diver?" she whispered.

She ran to him and hugged him, and then she began to cry, because she suddenly realized that *savior* was exactly the right word.

7

Peli-Ken's and Peli-Can'ts

Harold's going to be okay," Diver announced.

Marquez dropped the ancient copy of *National Geographic* she'd been thumbing through for the past half-hour. "Harold? You mean the pelican?"

Diver shrugged. "He felt like a Harold."

"Thank God. I didn't need that on my conscience."

An old man entered the waiting room. He was thoroughly bald, with a gold ring in one ear, and he was wearing a tattered Grateful Dead T-shirt. A pack of Marlboros poked from his breast pocket. Harold was in his arms, wrapped in a brown bath towel.

"You the perpetrator?" he asked Marquez.

"That's Ken," Diver explained.

Marquez moved to pet Harold, then reconsidered. "Is it mad?"

"Too dazed to be mad. Mad comes later. Broken clavicle. It'll be fine." Ken adjusted the blanket. "No thanks to you."

"It's not like I ran the bird down on purpose," Marquez said. She was feeling dazed herself, actually. The trailer that served as a makeshift hospital for Peli-Ken's was stifling, even with the antiquated fan in the corner going full speed.

And she was trying to absorb the bizarre fact that she was talking to *Diver*. Summer's Diver. Diver, the object of Marquez's ill-fated flirtation the previous summer. Diver, who was just possibly the most beautiful male in the continental United States.

Diver, who was, technically speaking, missing in action.

"We take donations. This is a nonprofit wildlife refuge. Costs like hell to fix one bird." Ken was clearly not one for small talk.

"I don't really—" Marquez looked sheepishly at Diver.

"MasterCard, Visa, Amex," Ken continued.

Harold gazed at her with bitter, beady eyes.

"Well, I do have this MasterCard," Marquez said, careful not to say "*my* MasterCard."

"Diver will take care of it," Ken said as he left.

"Bye, Harold," Marquez said, waving weakly.

Diver went behind a board on cement blocks

that served as a counter. He pulled out a little metal box with a credit card imprint machine.

Marquez watched him like someone in a dream. His skin was much darker than it had been when she'd seen him at Christmas, and his shimmering blond hair was shorter, the result of a recent parental mandate. Summer had written Marquez about *that* argument. He was thinner, too, but still taut with muscle. As usual, he was dressed in nothing but an old pair of swim trunks.

"I cannot believe I am standing here talking to you, Diver," Marquez said. "You *are* real, right? I mean, I'm not hallucinating because I missed lunch?"

Diver placed a credit card slip into the machine. He moved with a strange and deliberate grace that fascinated Marquez, who always moved at hyperspeed.

"It's me." He held out his hand for the credit card.

Marquez hesitated, then proffered it as nonchalantly as she could. Maybe he wouldn't notice the name. Diver was not one for details.

"But don't you think it's incredibly weird, us meeting up like this?"

Diver glanced at the card and slipped it into the machine without reaction. "Yeah. You hitting one of my pelicans and all."

"Your pelicans."

"Well, they're not anyone's pelicans, really."

Diver smiled at her. He had the most penetrating blue eyes.

Carefully Diver moved the arm of the imprint machine, then handed Marquez the card and slip.

Marquez stared at him. "Everybody's worried about you."

A pained look flickered across Diver's face. "That's not what I wanted."

"Maybe you should tell them where you are, you know?"

He looked at her—looked through her, actually. He had this way of gazing at you that was both innocent and deadly. Bambi with X-ray vision. "Do they know where you are?" he asked.

They. As though he and Marquez had a common enemy.

"I just can't deal with Summer and Diana and everybody right now. I was supposed to be with them this week. It's spring break. Come to think of it, you were supposed to be with them, too."

Diver winced. He passed Marquez a pen.

Marquez looked down at the credit card slip. She checked the signature on the back of the card. *Diana Olan,* she wrote, trying to approximate her friend's crisp penmanship.

"How much will it cost to fix up Harold?" she asked.

"Ken usually asks for fifty."

Marquez considered. How generous was Diana feeling? A hundred bucks' worth of guilt?

She made a donation of two hundred and fifty dollars.

Diver raised his eyes at the amount. "You're a generous woman, Diana," he said, without a hint of a smile.

Marquez smiled, though. "I won't tell them where you are," she said, "if you won't tell them where I am."

"Come on," he said, slowly shaking his head. "I'll show you where I live. But you can't tell anyone, okay?"

"I promise."

"You can stay for a while if you need a place."

He took her hand, and she was surprised how good it felt to touch someone, anyone, but especially him.

"I need a place," she said, and she knew he understood.

"Marquez is missing." Summer plopped down next to Austin on a bench. The Cinderella Castle loomed before her, a fantasy of slender towers and lacy filigree work. Earlier in the day Summer had thought it was enchanting, a fairy tale brought to life. But now, as the shadows lengthened and the sun prepared to set, it almost looked ominous.

"Marquez," Austin repeated. "This is the friend you were going to meet in Boca Beach?"

"With my cousin Diana." And my boyfriend,

69

Seth, she added silently. "I got Diana on her cell phone. She said Marquez just sort of vanished this morning. She left a note on her wall."

"Her wall?"

"Long story." Summer chewed on a thumbnail. "Diana said that Marquez's boyfriend broke up with her. Maybe she was upset about that."

Austin patted her knee. "I'm sure she'll be fine. She's probably just sorting things out. Sometimes people need to do that."

"I know. Marquez is pretty self-reliant. I don't think she'll do anything stupid. But still, I can't help worrying." She sighed. "This spring break isn't exactly starting out the way I'd planned."

"You mean me."

"Not exactly. Just . . . everything."

Austin jumped up. He handed Summer the mouse ears he'd bought for her. "One more picture," he said. "Before the sun goes."

"I feel like a complete idiot, Austin," she protested, but she put on the plastic mouse ears and grinned stupidly. Two children nearby giggled.

Austin advanced the film and stuffed the camera in his backpack. "You're very obliging," he said in a whisper. "I like that in a woman."

Summer did not smile. She did not feel like smiling. She yanked off the mouse ears and stared at them with contempt. They were a sign of her deep and abiding awfulness. They made her feel dirty.

She'd kissed a perfect stranger for no other reason than because she wanted to, and because he had really sweet, sad eyes and made her laugh. That morning she'd been promising herself she would never do anything to jeopardize her relationship with Seth, and then she'd gone right ahead and done something very jeopardizing. If that was a word.

"Are you okay?" Austin asked. "You've spoken, like, six words in the last hour."

"I am scum. There. That's three more."

"You are not scum. I would not fall for any woman who was even remotely scumlike."

"You have not fallen for me," Summer said in a harsh whisper. "You have kissed me, which was an unfortunate oversight on my part—"

"What with you having a boyfriend and all. Yes."

"Yes, what with Seth and all, and now I have to spend the next few days with him pretending nothing ever happened." The reality hit her like a sharp slap. "Not just a few days, but weeks, months. Years. What if we get married? What if I have to go to my grave with this horrible secret, never telling a single living soul?"

"It's not like you killed me. You just kissed me."

"I am scum. No, I'm less than scum."

"Scum lite?"

Summer glared at him. "This is not funny. Not to me, Austin."

Austin gazed at her thoughtfully. He seemed to be considering his words with great care.

"Summer, you're about to go back to the airport and get on your plane, and I am never, ever going to see you again. Okay? And this will just be something that happened between two people who needed each other for a moment. And frankly, it's something I will cherish, even if you won't."

"I didn't need it. I was just kissed in Minneapolis. I'm not some . . . some nymphomaniac—"

"*I* needed it. Not like *needed* needed. I . . . some writer I am, huh? I'm out of words." Austin brushed his hand past his eyes. "I needed to be with someone for a while."

Summer heard the throaty catch in his voice. "What do you mean, *I'm* about to get on that plane? What about you?"

Austin shook his head slightly. "There's been a change of plans."

"I *knew* you were afraid to fly!" she said triumphantly. "I promise that if you just do deep breathing and stuff, you'll be fine, Austin, and . . ." She lost steam and sighed. "Oh."

"What?"

"For a minute there I forgot I was scum. Pond scum. Toilet bowl scum. Scum on the floor of the mildewy showers in the locker rooms at school—"

Austin laughed suddenly. He reached for

Summer's hands and kissed them both, one at a time, solemnly and carefully. A middle-aged woman walking past with a toddler in tow looked as though she was about to swoon.

"Summer Smith, you have lightened a dark moment in my life, and for that I will be eternally grateful."

Summer blinked. Was he serious? What was he talking about? "Austin," she said, "I realize you said no questions, but I have to know—what's going *on* with you? The running off the plane, and the secrets, and now you're not even finishing your trip. Tell me. You can't turn me to scum and then run off without ever letting me know."

Austin rubbed his eyes. Suddenly he looked impossibly tired. "I'm going to tell you this so you'll let it go, okay?" he said at last. "It's real simple. My dad has this . . . this disease, this bad disease. It's called Huntington's, and it kills you, but before it kills you it makes your life a living hell for years." He swallowed. "He's in Boca Beach, in a hospital there."

"So that's where you were going, to see him?" Summer said gently. "And now you're having second thoughts? I can understand that, Austin, but you have to know how much it would mean to him—"

"I don't know that," Austin snapped. "I haven't seen him in years, not since that time I told you about, here, at Disney World. And now he's so bad off, he probably won't even recognize me, so I'm kind of starting to think this is not the best idea I've ever had."

They sat quietly for a while in the waning light. Clumps of tired children marched past. Toddlers dozed in their parents' arms or in strollers filled with Disney souvenirs. The air was still warm and sweetly scented.

Summer closed her eyes. She felt muddled inside, a confusion of feelings that made her wish she could be someone else for just a minute or two. Long enough, anyway, to get a perspective on the day. She'd climbed onto the plane that morning intending to leave her worries behind, but now she'd just acquired more. She was worried about Marquez. She was worried about Austin and his father. She was worried about her feelings—was that what they were?—for Austin. And, of course, she was worried about Diver.

She glanced at Austin. He was gazing at the castle, lost in private thoughts. She tried to imagine what he must be going through. His worries were so much bigger than hers. What if it were her own dad in that hospital room?

Without thinking, she reached for Austin's hand. "I'll go with you," she said suddenly.

"What? Where?"

"To the hospital. To see your dad."

"No way, Summer. This isn't your problem."

"Well, for some strange reason, it feels like it is now."

Austin leaned back against the bench and shook his head slowly. "No."

"Austin, I want to help you with this."

"You want to help the very person who's turned you to scum?"

Summer shrugged. "Ironic, isn't it?" She stood, grabbed his hands, and pulled him to his feet. "Come on. You have to go back to the airport anyway. You left your stuff in the locker there. It'll be okay, Austin. We'll fly to Boca, and then you can come see the yacht and meet Diana. I told her I'd just take a cab to the marina when I got to the airport, it'll be so late and all. Then, in the morning, I'll meet you at your motel and we'll go to the hospital together."

"Summer." Austin stood firm. "I don't want to do this."

"You wouldn't have come this far if you didn't want to." She smiled. "Don't think about tomorrow. We'll just deal with the plane, then take it from there."

He closed his eyes, then opened them, gazing at her with intense curiosity. "Why are you doing this?"

"I don't know," she admitted. "I just know I'll feel worse if I leave you here than if you come with me." She took his hand, twining their fingers together. "Scum or no scum."

8

Hanky-panky on the Hanky-panky

"This cannot be the right place," Austin declared as he and Summer got out of the cab.

Summer checked a piece of paper. "Boca Beach Yacht Club, pier nineteen, slip seven. The *Hanky-panky*."

Austin rolled his eyes.

"I told you, this boat belongs to my aunt Mallory's best friend, who's an even more famous romance novelist than Mallory is. She, like, wears mink nightgowns and stuff."

"Apparently it pays to sell out," Austin said. "Maybe I should give up poetry and go into bodice rippers."

They began walking past the long docks. The water lapped softly against the piers. A long string of condominiums stretched out along the beach. Yellow lights glowed from the floor-to-ceiling windows. Here and there on the sand, groups of spring breakers were huddled, laughing and talking. Someone was playing a guitar.

It was beautiful and romantic, and Seth should have been there. Summer felt a guilty twinge. She'd been twinging all evening. But each time she told herself the same thing: She was helping Austin get through a tough time. She would go with him to the hospital the next day and then that would be the end of it.

"The thing is, Summer," Austin said, "these are not boats. These are *Lifestyles of the Disgustingly Rich and Undeservedly Famous* yachts."

"I think we've gone too far." Summer paused to scan the long rows of huge yachts.

"Summer! Over here!"

Summer spun around. At the end of a long pier, she could just make out a female figure, waving. "Diana!" she called back.

"Finally, you made it! Hurry up!"

"Can you believe the size of that thing?" Summer asked Austin as she started down the pier. "It's like something Donald Trump would own."

Austin took her arm. "Summer, maybe I should get going."

"No way. You've been depressed ever since

we got back on the plane. Come on. I want you to meet Diana and see the yacht. Diana's got her car. We'll drive you over to the motel in a while."

Diana was waiting for them on the wide deck. She had on a yellow bathing suit top and cutoffs and looked, as usual, cover-model gorgeous. Her dark hair was pulled into a loose ponytail.

"Welcome to the Love Boat," Diana announced. She reached for a switch, and instantly the entire yacht came alive with little white twinkling lights. A nice reggae tune, perfect island music, started playing from an elaborate sound system.

They climbed aboard. Diana gave Summer a long, warm hug—surprisingly warm for Diana, who was not the most affectionate person on the planet.

"And who might this be?" Diana asked, turning to Austin.

"This is Austin Reed. My seatmate."

Austin shook Diana's hand. Diana hung on a moment longer than was strictly necessary. "And you're the reason Summer missed her plane?" Diana asked.

"Guilty as charged."

"It's just as well," Diana said, taking Summer's bag from her. "I was running late, no thanks to Marquez, and it gave me a chance to get things ready. Come see."

"Diana," Summer said as they followed her down a teak stairway, "this is so . . . amazingly cool."

"Mallory has excellent taste in friends. Although the same can't necessarily be said for her friends." She opened the first cabin door. "Exhibit A."

Summer gasped. The huge stateroom featured a heart-shaped king-size bed covered with a pink satin comforter. As a matter of fact, everything in the room seemed to be made of pink satin.

"Sort of a retro whorehouse theme," Austin commented.

"Would you expect anything less from the author of *Hot Nights, Skin to Skin*?"

Summer picked up a vase filled with pink roses. "The roses are from me," Diana said. "I figured this would be your room, Summer . . . or yours and Seth's, or yours and whoever's . . ."

Summer felt a blush sizzle her cheeks. "Wrong, Diana," she said quickly, casting an embarrassed glance at Austin. "Seth and I aren't . . . you know."

"And she and whoever aren't either," Austin offered.

"Okay, I get it. But wait," Diana said. "There's more. *Now* what would you pay?"

She led them back to the upper deck to a heart-shaped Jacuzzi, also pink. Shiny Mylar balloons danced in the light breeze. Each one read *Happy SB!*

"SB?" Austin inquired.

"Spring break," Summer said. She hugged Diana. "You shouldn't have gone to all this trouble."

"I didn't mind. It was kind of fun. Sort of like getting a second chance at my senior year." She shrugged. "I kind of went through that period in a daze."

"Didn't we all?" Austin said with a smile.

"So." Diana sat on the edge of the Jacuzzi. "Here's the deal. We have this whole boat to ourselves for the week, courtesy of Mallory and her buddy, Deirdre. It's stocked to overflowing with every food item known to man. On the beach, we have a nonstop party going on. This place is even better than Fort Lauderdale. It's not quite so overrun with puking frat boys, but there's still plenty of, um, raw material. In fact, there's this lifeguard . . . but I digress." She snapped her fingers. "Oh, yeah. They're doing an MTV shoot here this week. You know, a live show from spring break or some such thing. It's party central, and we've got front row seats."

"Amazing," Summer murmured.

"The only down side is that Mallory managed to saddle us with a chaperon of sorts." She pointed to the yacht berthed next to theirs. A burly man wearing a skipper's cap waved. "That's Jack," Diana explained. "He's a retired cop who married money. He's informed me he'll be keeping an eye

81

on things. He knows how we kids can get a little carried away." She grinned. "So, what's the plan? You two hungry?"

"Summer," Austin said, looking uncomfortable, "I think maybe I'll head for the motel."

"Motel?" Diana cast Austin a flirtatious smile. "We've got plenty of room right here, especially with Marquez and Seth gone. You can stay here. After all, we have our very own in-house cop keeping an eye on things."

Austin was looking off at the sparkling sky, lost in thought. "I don't want to crash your party, Summer."

"Stay, Austin," Summer said. "It'll make it easier in the morning, when we . . . go."

Diana cast her a questioning look, which Summer chose to ignore.

Austin sighed. He looked battle-weary and depressed, and Summer wondered if she'd made a mistake by insisting that he finish the trip. "I am beat. Maybe I'll take you up on the offer after all, if you're sure you're okay with it."

"Positive," Summer said.

Austin gave a tired smile. "Which cabin should I take?"

"Well, we have the Love Song, the Love Letter, and the Love Nest. I kid you not. She named each one after one of her books. Oh, yeah, I forgot Love Potion."

Austin shrugged.

"Go with Potion. It's the only one with white sheets."

"Thanks." Austin turned to Summer. He gave her a lingering kiss on the cheek. "I owe you."

Summer glanced at Diana, who raised her brows and crossed her arms over her chest. Summer knew what that look meant. It meant she would be doing a lot of explaining, real soon.

"Okay, give. Start at the beginning, and I do mean the beginning."

Summer lay back in the Jacuzzi and sighed. The night air was cool on her face and shoulders. Across the water, students were dancing on the beach around a small fire. The music floated back to the marina in bits and pieces.

Summer gazed across the bubbling water at her cousin. Diana's face was damp and glowing. She'd been so great to Summer since she'd arrived, helping her unpack, fixing her a snack. And then there were the roses and the balloons. . . . Summer felt a little bad thinking this, but it was strange. Diana was not the most generous, open person in the world. She was being *awfully* nice to Summer. Of course, people changed. She hadn't seen Diana in a while, not since Christmas.

She wished Marquez were there. Marquez would know. She had a nuclear-powered BS detector built into her brain.

"What are we going to do about Marquez?" Summer asked.

"You're evading my question." Diana sighed. "I don't know what to do about Marquez, the lowlife. She's messing up our vacation. She leaves some cryptic note on her wall, rips off my credit card—"

"She might have done that by mistake."

"You are too nice for your own good, Summer."

Not so nice, Summer thought. Actually, I'm scum.

"Anyway," Diana continued, "I don't know what to do. I've called every friend of hers I could think of. I drove to all her usual hangouts." She slipped lower into the water and propped her feet on the far side of the Jacuzzi. "You know how freaked Marquez gets when she's got emotional stuff to deal with. The weird thing is, when she and I went shopping last night she seemed okay." She hesitated. "I mean, I *thought* she was okay. Am I, like, the lousiest friend on the planet? I should know these things, shouldn't I?"

"Marquez is really hard to read," Summer assured her. "Remember when you guys came up over Christmas and she was mad because she thought Diver was ignoring her, but nobody knew till we dragged it out of her?"

"Yeah." Diana looked uncomfortable. "Christmas. We were all pretty weirded out over the holidays, I guess."

Summer wondered what she meant. "I thought the holidays were great. Diver was a little off, though. . . ." Her voice trailed away. "My parents were putting so much pressure on him for it to be perfect."

"It's just that sometimes . . . I don't think about other people's feelings like I should." Diana stared straight at Summer, as if she was telling her something vital. "You know?"

Summer didn't, but she nodded anyway.

They sat in silence for a while, listening to the music and the gentle slap of the waves against the hull.

"So, what *is* the deal with Austin?" Diana asked with a sly grin. "Thought I'd forget, didn't you?"

"There is no deal. We met on the plane. We missed our connection and killed time at Disney World. His dad's sick, and he's going to the hospital tomorrow to see him. End of story."

"The way he kissed you didn't look like the end of the story to me."

"On the cheek, Diana."

"But with feeling." Diana sat up. "That was a cheek kiss that was hoping to be a lips kiss." She paused. "You know, if you *did* have a little thing going with Austin, it's not like Seth would ever have to know."

"We didn't have a thing, whatever that is. And we're not going to. I'm just trying to help him, is all."

"He's got incredible eyes. Reminds me of Ethan Hawke, sort of—"

"Drop it, Diana."

She grinned slyly. "I hope I didn't complicate matters, inviting him to stay here."

"It's fine, really. He'll be gone tomorrow."

"And Seth will be here the day after that," Diana added. "He's so psyched about this week, I can't believe it."

"Seth?" Summer asked in surprise. "When did you talk to Seth?"

Diana hesitated. "Um, this morning. He called me."

"Why?"

"Oh, you know Seth. Ever vigilant. He wanted to be sure I had your flight number and arrival time."

Summer felt another guilt twinge. Typical Seth, always looking out for her. While she was busy behaving in scumlike ways behind his back.

But was it scumlike to want to help out Austin? Hadn't she guided him through a difficult moment that day? It felt kind of nice, taking care of someone. Seth was always so busy taking care of her. Checking the air in her tires, making sure she had a warm enough coat. That kind of thing.

"Summer?"

"Hmm?"

"I'm glad you're here."

"Me, too, Diana. I wish Marquez were here with us."

"Yeah. I hate to admit it, but I do, too. Summer?"

"Hmm?"

"My toes are starting to wrinkle. If we don't get out of this Jacuzzi soon, we'll be shriveled-up prune women."

Summer giggled. "Five more minutes, okay?" she said.

"Five more. What the heck. It's your spring break, after all."

9

Night Dancing, Night Swimming, and Other Dangerous Sports

"I can't believe you live in a tree," Marquez said for what had to be the hundredth time that evening.

Diver stretched out on the rough wooden floor beside her. "Tree house," he corrected.

"It's so *you* somehow," Marquez said. "Last summer you spent more time on top of Summer's stilt house than in it."

She took in the small room, built of rough boards, nestled high in the arms of two large pines about a hundred yards from the water's edge. One wall was actually a floor-to-ceiling bamboo matchstick blind that rolled up to reveal an unobstructed view of the ocean. A small camp stove sat on a tiny folding table in one corner. Underneath was an ice chest. On a shelf by the open doorway were a plate and utensils, a metal cup, and a roll of toilet paper. An outhouse by Ken's trailer served as the bathroom, and a sleeping bag on the floor was Diver's bed.

"Ken lived here for years," Diver said. "But then his leg went bad on him and he couldn't climb up the ladder. So now I live here."

Marquez stared at Diver. She still couldn't quite believe he was lying next to her. In the soft glow of yellow moonlight, he looked especially beautiful. She would love to paint him, to capture the way his muscles wove in and out, to catch the luminous glow in his eyes. On her wall mural there was a spot . . . but no. That would be gone soon.

"Thanks for dinner," Diver said, taking a last swig of orange juice out of a small glass bottle. Marquez had driven Diver to the nearest food source, a Shell station on the highway. They'd splurged on junk food, all courtesy of Diana's gold card. It was getting quite a workout.

"Doritos, Oreos, and Chee-tos. I do love to cook."

They lay on Diver's sleeping bag, watching the moon frost the gentle waves. The warm breeze carried the sharp tang of the ocean. A handful of seagulls huddled below the tree house.

"Just tell me this, Diver," Marquez said. "How did you end up here, of all places? It's perfectly you—the birds, the tree house, the complete Diverness of it all—but how?"

"It just sort of found me."

"Why can't I do that?" Marquez wondered. "Just land in the right place. God knows I try. I tried like crazy to just sort of let Princeton and Yale find me, but they weren't taking the hint."

"So you'll go somewhere else."

"Oh, sure, FCU wants me—you know, Florida Coastal, the artsy-fartsy one where all the students dress in black. But I want to be a lawyer, Diver, and lawyers do not go to artsy-fartsy colleges. They go to Yale."

Diver cast her a gentle, affectionate smile. Looking into his eyes was like staring into a mirror with great lighting, Marquez thought. You *seemed* just a little better than you knew you really were.

"But you're an artist," he said.

She felt herself get angry, then let it go. It was impossible to get angry at Diver, and besides, he was just saying the same thing everyone else said. It was her destiny, blah, blah, blah. Well, she was going to make her own destiny. So what if she'd gotten rejection letters from a couple of snotty Northeastern colleges? She felt tears coming and fought them. So what if she'd been rejected by the guy she'd thought she loved?

She touched Diver's hand, and he seemed surprised. Not like J.T., who, from their first date, had taken the slightest touch as a sign she was hot for him. He'd been right, of course.

"Tell me the truth. How'd you end up here? Summer said she figured you'd end up back in Florida, but why here?"

At the mention of Summer's name, Diver looked back at the ocean. "I hitched down the coast," he said. "And I got a job driving a diaper-service truck—"

"No way."

"It wasn't so bad. There was this big stork on the side of it, and all the mothers seemed really glad to see me."

"I'll bet."

"But then one day I came across this egret by the side of the road, hurt real bad. Someone told me about Ken, and eventually he offered me a job. I get room and board and the use of the truck, and I get to help him with the birds."

"No pay?"

Diver shrugged. "I have a little. From . . . be-fore."

"So you went from a truck with a stork on it to a truck with a pelican on it. Very upwardly mobile."

"I like it," Diver said, a little defensively. "There's no pressure. I've had enough pressure."

"I like your style, Diver. Escape. Just hide out."

He looked startled. "I'm not hiding. I'm just not there anymore." He didn't have to say

"Bloomington, Minnesota." Marquez knew where "there" was.

Diver rolled onto his side. "Is that what you're doing, Marquez? Running?"

His bluntness surprised her. "Things got out of control, you know? School stuff, and my dad's selling the house, and . . . and J.T. The usual suspects."

Marquez cleared her throat, hoping he didn't see the tears pooling in her eyes yet again. She listened to the waves whisper as they came and went, hush, hush, like a warning not to talk too much. It was too quiet there, way too quiet.

She jumped to her feet. "I have an idea."

"What?"

"Meet me on the beach. We're having ourselves a party."

The sand was cool on Marquez's bare feet. The beach was empty except for some hyperactive sandpipers. Diver was sitting by the water's edge, the foamy surf licking his legs.

"Everything we need," Marquez announced. She held up the six-pack she'd conned the Shell clerk into letting her buy. In her other hand she had her portable stereo. "What'll it be? How about some Janet Jackson? 'Runaway,' that'd hit the spot."

"I like the ocean, actually."

"Can't dance to the ocean," Marquez said.

She was starting to feel it again, that coiled-up feeling in her limbs that made her want to jump back into her car and floor the accelerator. It was because she was thinking. She'd let J.T. crawl back into her brain, and that was her mistake. Well, the beer would take care of that. Beer and Diver and dancing. The cure for what ailed her.

She unscrewed a top and handed the beer to Diver, but he shook his head. She took a nice long swallow. It was lukewarm, but what the hell. Then she got on her knees and popped Janet into the CD player.

"I thought you didn't drink," Diver said, sounding disappointed in her.

"I don't. But today's a special occasion. Today I ran away from the world and ran straight into you." She cranked up the volume. "I hope these batteries hold up. Of course, I can always charge more at Shell."

"Does Diana know?"

"About the card? Diana who-only-leaves-her-coffin-at-night Olan?"

"I thought you were friends," Diver said simply.

God, he was making this hard. "I'm going to pay her back every penny, okay? And you know she's made of money. She's got, like, three hundred gold cards. She's got gold and platinum and that one Ringo Starr designed. So it's not like she's out on the street begging."

Marquez turned up the volume some more, but no matter how high she went, the sound was swallowed up in the deep night. She took another long swig of beer.

"Come on, Diver, dance with me."

"I don't dance."

"Of course you dance. Everyone dances."

She took his hand, but he just sat there on the sand. Marquez began to move to the music. "You're just shy," she said, taking another swallow. "Summer was that way too when she first got here, remember? Maybe it's a family trait."

At the mention of Summer's name, Diver looked away.

Damn. Why was she bringing her up? Stop it. Diver did not want to think about Summer, and Marquez did not want to think about J.T., and the only way to be sure of that was for Marquez to shut her mouth and just move.

She put down her beer and changed the CD. Then she went back to Diver, took his hands, and pulled him up. He grinned. "You'll be sorry."

"I doubt it."

Marquez inched closer and let her hands slip loosely around his taut waist. Mazzy Star was singing "Fade Into You." It was dreamy and moody, the rhythm slipping into Marquez's muscles and blood and taking over. She kept her feet almost still, since Diver seemed determined not to move, and just let the rest of her body roll with the music.

"It's easy," she said. "It's like . . . you know when you're on a raft, and the waves kind of just roll under you and your whole body moves along?"

Diver cocked his head. He was looking at her torso, watching it sway and undulate, with a sort of detached, scientific curiosity. Marquez moved a little closer, and he began to move with her. He closed his eyes and moved with perfect, easy grace, the way she'd known he would.

Halfway through the song, the batteries gave out.

Diver opened his eyes and looked at her. "The waves are music, too," he pointed out. They kept dancing.

After a while Marquez put her head on his shoulder. It was smooth and cool. His neck smelled, somehow, of the ocean. She let her fingers tangle in his hair. It was very soft, like a child's.

They were touching now, her breasts against his smooth chest, their legs intertwined. She closed her eyes and tried to feel the beer in her blood, but there wasn't nearly enough. She moved her lips until she touched his neck, and lingered there in what might or might not have been a kiss. A sweet shiver of longing shot through her. It was the signal for Diver to bend down, to meet her lips, to kiss her until she forgot all about the things J.T. had said to her, but Diver just stared out at the ocean. His hands were around her waist, loosely, noncommittally, not the way her hands were roaming over his shoulders and chest.

It wasn't fair. She was sending all the right signals. Any guy with half a libido would have gotten the message by now. He'd ignored her this way at Christmas, too, although then all she'd attempted was some conversation. This was worse, far worse. She could tell he was about to say something embarrassing to her. Why didn't he just kiss her? Why didn't he know what she wanted?

Diver touched her cheek, the place where a tear was slowly trickling. "It's hard when you lose someone you love," he whispered.

She began to sob, great, sad sobs from someplace dark inside her. They stopped dancing, and Diver held her very close and let her cry, and she realized suddenly that he had known what she'd wanted after all.

Summer woke with a jolt. Her mouth tasted sour, and her stomach seemed to be rocking back and forth like a swing. No, *she* was rocking back and forth. She was in a water bed on a boat on the water. For the weak of stomach, this did not seem to be the best combination in the world.

She climbed out of bed. If she was going to be sick, no sense in doing it on Deirdre's pink satin sheets. She was surprised at how warm the air was, even in her baby-tee and boxers. Back in Minnesota, you didn't get out of bed in March without long underwear and a fleece robe. Better yet, you just didn't get out of bed till June.

She tiptoed to the upper deck. The water lapped softly against the hulls of the great yachts. Diana had left the twinkle lights on, and their reflections floated on the black water like swimming stars. Behind her, the condos and yachts and hotels were clumped together, fortresslike, a bastion against the great black question mark that was the ocean.

How many times the previous summer had she and Diver spent nights like this, sitting side by side, awed and silenced by the vastness of the water? Until now she hadn't realized how much she'd missed it. Minnesota was the land of ten thousand lakes, they said, but a lake was something you could get your mind around. The ocean was humbling and yet strangely soothing. Was Diver near the ocean now, perhaps watching it that night the way she was? The thought made her angry. He'd run off, leaving her parents and Summer to clean up the mess. He didn't deserve the soothing sounds of the waves. He didn't deserve any peace.

He hadn't tried to make things work. Sure, it

was hard to reconnect with a family you'd lost—Summer could understand that much, at least. It was only natural he'd miss his freedom a little. But in return for following a few rules, for going back to school and cutting his hair and showing up for dinner, he'd gotten the love he deserved. And then he'd run out on it after just a few months, and for what? Warmer temperatures and some palm trees?

For the ocean, she told herself, drinking in the familiar, intoxicating scent of the water. For that, she could almost—almost—understand.

Something caught her eye far out in the water. A dolphin, maybe? A gull?

She watched the round black shape, vaguely curious, and yawned. She should go back to sleep. She would have a big day of doing nothing the next day. Dozing on the beach, eating funnel cakes on the boardwalk, maybe doing some jet-skiing later.

But first, of course, she would go with Austin to the hospital. Then he would move on, and Seth would come, and the guilty twinges would go away. It would be nice when Seth got there. Like old times. Maybe they could do some scuba diving, the way they had during the summer. They would kiss and dance and eat and kiss and sun and swim and kiss, and had she mentioned kiss?

She hoped Marquez would show up by then.

She hoped Austin would be gone by then.

The black dot grew smaller. Probably a gull, she decided. With a sigh, Summer headed back downstairs. She was almost to her cabin when she noticed that Austin's door was half open. She knocked on it softly. When there was no answer, she pushed the door open all the way.

Austin was gone. His bed was still made. His guitar and backpack sat in one corner.

Summer's pulse quickened. Where was he? Had he left the boat, maybe gone for a walk on the docks?

The galley. Maybe he was just fixing himself a snack. She rushed to the spacious kitchen. No Austin.

Summer returned to the deck. She scanned the lighted docks for signs of movement, but all was still.

Suddenly she spun around, eyes darting across the black horizon. She looked for the tiny dot, moving slowly and deliberately across the water toward a destination that could not be reached.

At last she found it. After a moment it vanished, lost beneath the water. Her heart stopped.

It resurfaced at last.

She ran to the dinghy tied to the back of the yacht. Her hands were trembling as she loosened the thick, wet rope.

10

Dark Water and Darker Truths

*I*t took several long minutes to get the dinghy in the water and more to get the little engine going. Summer was glad she'd spent time on boats during the summer. Otherwise she would have struggled for days to get the outboard humming.

She took off in the direction of the small, dark figure. The waves were gentle, but she caught enough of them head-on to make for a bumpy ride. The cold salt spray stung her face, and soon she was shivering.

She was dashing to the rescue, dressed in nothing but a wet T-shirt and a damp pair of boxers. It occurred to her that Austin might well be in town, having a fine old time, while she was out there rescuing a sea gull or a figment of her warped imagination.

The dot, a little bigger now, slipped again into the water, then reappeared. The moon hid behind a ridge of clouds, and the water went blacker still. She lost sight of whatever it was she was chasing.

Summer kept going, hoping against hope she was heading in the right direction. The moon reappeared. Again she located the dot, and this time she was close enough to see that it really was human. Arms flailed in an attempt at a crawl stroke.

"Austin!" she yelled, but her voice was lost in the roar of the motor. "Austin! Hang on!"

He kept going, struggling against the waves. She realized with a shock that he was still moving away from her. Hadn't he heard the motor? Hadn't he seen her? Was he *trying* to drown?

Slowly, bouncing over each wave in the tiny boat, Summer approached him. She could make out his dark hair. His shoulders caught the moonlight. She could see his hands grabbing at the water in aimless, desperate strokes.

"I'm coming!" she screamed, and this time he glanced over his shoulder for a split second. She could glimpse enough of his face to tell he didn't want her there.

Again he disappeared beneath the water. As he went down, the look on his face was almost peaceful. Summer moved the boat close to the spot where he'd vanished and waited for him to reappear, the way he had before.

The waves slapped the boat, urging it from the spot. The moon slipped away again.

"Austin!" She screamed it, but there was no response.

She was torn between all-out panic and anger. The jerk. She was not a strong swimmer, and now she was going to drown trying to save his sorry butt.

Summer took a deep breath and dove. The water clutched at her with icy hands. She opened her eyes and struggled to fight the current, which was much stronger than she'd expected. She could see nothing. She was a fool. She was going to freeze to death. She was going to freeze or drown or maybe both, for some stranger she'd never met. She stroked again and again, and her lungs were hurting, and the cold was hurting, she was an idiot, and now she'd ruined her spring vacation totally, and Seth would kill her, except that she'd already be dead—

She hit something with her head, hard. It gave way slowly, and she reached out and saw white and touched something, an arm far too cold to be flesh. She grabbed it tightly and held on and pulled, and then she was heading up, because up meant air, and air was all she cared about.

After a moment Austin seemed to come to life. She felt something cold on her waist and realized it was his hands, and now it was him saving her, pushing her, pulling her toward the surface, where there would be air. Just one good lungful of air. That was all she wanted.

They broke the surface, Summer first. She sucked in so much air it hurt, gasping and sputtering as a wave closed over her head. Austin was beside her, barely treading. She reached for his hand. "Come on," she managed, and they began to half-swim, half-tread toward the boat.

The dinghy had drifted far away, and even the small waves exerted a tremendous pull. They swam side by side, wordlessly, until they neared the little boat. After two attempts, Summer was able to clutch the side. She hung on, dangling weakly, then, with a final burst of effort, threw her legs over the side. "Hurry," she said, her teeth chattering uncontrollably. Austin's eyes were closed. He rose and fell with a big wave.

"Damn it, Austin, you can't drown now!" Summer cried. "You'll ruin my spring break."

His eyes fluttered open. He managed the ghost of a smile.

Summer smiled back. She stretched out her hand.

He took it.

They were silent all the way home. Summer was too confused to ask any questions, and besides, she was too cold to talk. Her whole body exploded in spasms of shaking. Her teeth were chattering like a pair of wind-up dentures from a novelty store.

Austin sat in the bow. His head was in his hands. He was wearing a pair of cutoffs and nothing else. His skin was beyond pale, the translucent blue-white of skim milk.

When they reached the yacht, Summer was grateful that Diana was still asleep. The last thing she needed was a cross-examination right at that moment. And from the look of Austin, it was the last thing he needed as well.

She tied up the dinghy as best she could. Her arms ached. She was shocked at her weariness.

Austin climbed into the yacht with great effort. He looked as if he might pass out at any second. Summer slipped her arm around his waist. As cold as she was, he was even colder.

She took him to her cabin because it was farther away from Diana's, and Summer didn't want her to hear them and wake. She helped Austin sit on the bed and wrapped the silk comforter around his shoulders. In the closet she found a pair of pink terry robes embroidered in red with *His* and *Hers*.

She handed one of the robes to Austin. "I'm going to go change in the bathroom," she said. "Put this on."

Summer took her overnight bag and went into the bathroom. She put on the warmest clothes she'd brought, a pair of jeans, some socks, and a long-sleeved T-shirt, and then on top of that she put the robe. She took a long time drying her hair.

She knocked before opening the bathroom door.

"Yeah," Austin said. "It's okay."

Austin was still sitting on the edge of the water bed, although now he was wearing the ridiculous pink robe.

"I can't stop shivering," he said.

"Me either." She sat on the other side of the water bed, sending a gentle ripple across the mattress. "The water bed's really warm," she said, crawling under the comforter. She pulled the covers up to her chin.

After a moment Austin joined her. They lay side by side, swathed in pink. Slowly the warmth of the water bed, the comforter, and the robes began to penetrate. Summer looked over at Austin. He was staring at the mural painted on the ceiling. It was from the cover of one of Deirdre's books and featured a lovesick Indian and a woman with a three-inch waist.

"I'm sorry."

His voice was so low she could barely hear him. Summer rolled onto her side, her head propped up on her hand.

"Sorry? You swim halfway to Europe, and you're sorry?" Suddenly she realized how angry she was. "I could have drowned—you could have drowned, Austin! What were you *doing*?"

He reached out and gently let his fingers, still icy, trail along her cheek. "God, if anything had happened to you, I would never have forgiven myself."

"Well, it really wouldn't have been an issue, since you most likely would have been pretty dead yourself."

They fell silent. Summer flopped onto her back. The water bed made a gentle rippling noise.

"I just don't understand," Summer said at last. "Were you . . . trying to kill yourself?"

Austin gave a self-deprecating laugh. "If I was, it had to be the most inefficient suicide attempt in history."

"Austin," Summer said, "I know you said no questions, but I have to know. What's wrong? This is about more than your dad, isn't it? It isn't fair not to tell me."

"Life, it turns out, dear Summer, is not entirely fair."

"I saw something about an appointment written down in your notebook. For a clinic. And I was wondering—"

Austin sighed. "I wasn't just going to visit my dad, Summer," he said, biting off the words. "I was going to have some tests done."

"Tests?"

He looked away. "I don't want to talk about this."

"I just saved your damn life, Austin. You kind of owe me."

"Fine. You want to know? I'll tell you, then. Huntington's disease is genetic, Summer. There's a fifty-fifty chance I'll get it. My mom wants me to find out. I *thought* I wanted to find out." He took in a long, slow lungful of air. "But it turns out I don't want to know the future, since there's every chance the future sucks. It's kind of ironic, really. My mom and dad are divorced, and he and I were never that close. Now I'm worried we might be a lot closer than I ever realized."

Summer stared at Austin, speechless. "I don't know what to say," she whispered. She realized she was shivering again. "Even if you do have it, Austin . . . it doesn't show up until you're older, right? There could be a cure soon. They're doing all kinds of work with genes and stuff."

"That thought has occurred to me in my more optimistic moments."

"And maybe you don't even have it."

"And maybe I do." He rubbed his eyes. "Would you want to know?"

"I don't know. I guess maybe. If I knew, I could plan. Like maybe if I wanted to have kids, I'd reconsider. Or if I wanted to be a doctor, something that really takes a lot of school, then maybe I'd do something else instead." She nodded, only half convinced. "Yeah, so I guess I would want to know."

Austin smiled knowingly. "But suppose you forgo your dream of becoming a doctor or having kids, and then it turns out they do come up with a cure. You've abandoned the most important part of you, your dreams, and then fate comes along and goes, 'Sorry, you guessed wrong.'"

Summer chewed on a thumbnail. "Or suppose you think you'll have it someday, so you make all these changes, and then"—she snapped her fingers—"pow, you're hit by an ice cream truck when you're twenty-one."

"I'm just curious here. Why an ice cream truck?"

"I don't know. I guess it seemed more ironic."

Austin laughed softly, and Summer laughed with him. He took her hand and kissed it. "Summer, you are quite wonderful, do you know that? Thank you for dragging my stupid butt out of the ocean. I'm grateful. I think."

She felt tears coming, and she didn't even know why. "It's all so unfair, Austin," she said. "It's like one of those really horrible word problems in math where every time you think you have the answer, you come up with some other complication. I mean, I can't even decide which college to go to. I can't even decide which bathing suit to buy. The other day it took me five minutes to decide if I wanted sausage or bacon on my Egg McMuffin."

Austin stroked the back of her hand. His fingers were still cold and trembling slightly.

"And then," she added with a laugh, "I had a container of orange juice instead."

"I wish it were that simple."

"Maybe your parents can help. Or . . . do you have any brothers or sisters?"

"An older brother. He already had the test done."

"And?"

"And he's drawing up a will, if that gives you any indication. His fiancée's totally freaked."

A sudden wave of weariness came over Summer without warning. She was so tired, and this was all so impossibly sad and impossibly complicated. But she couldn't just ask Austin to go back to his dark cabin alone, not after all that had happened.

"You're still shivering," she said. "I'll go make some tea. You think they have tea?"

"I'll drink anything as long as it's not pink."

When she returned with two cups of steaming tea, Austin was reading her book of poems.

"It's chamomile." Summer placed the cups on the nightstand. "They had Red Zinger, but I thought you might object."

Austin accepted a cup gratefully. He took a long sip, then set his tea aside and slumped against his pillow. "I have a sort of favor to ask," he said.

Uh-oh, Summer told herself, you should have known. You let a guy, even a possibly suicidal one, into your satin-sheeted, heart-shaped water bed, and he's bound to get ideas.

Austin passed her the book of poems. "Could you maybe read one or two to me?" he asked softly.

She almost laughed. "You want me to read to you?"

He nodded, then closed his eyes. There were dark, shiny circles under his eyes. With his skin so pale, his damp hair, his half-grown beard, she could almost imagine him sick—if not right at that moment, then someday. Or, like his dad a few miles away, even dying.

"What should I read?"

"Doesn't matter."

She thumbed through the pages. At last she came to one that didn't seem too personal. She sat on a chair near the bed.

"'How sweet the moonlight sleeps upon this bank!'" she read, feeling slightly stupid.

"Shakespeare," Austin said softly, his eyes still closed. "He's not bad, for a dead guy." He opened one eye. "You know, if I weren't potentially genetically cursed, and if you didn't have a boyfriend named Seth, I'd probably kiss you right now." He closed his eye again.

Summer cleared her throat. She began to read again:

111

Here will we sit, and let the sound of music
Creep in our ears: soft stillness, and the night,
Become the touches of sweet harmony.

She looked over at Austin. He was sound asleep. A lock of hair had fallen over his eyes. She brushed it away gently. He did not stir.

Summer got up, closed the door behind her, and went up to the deck. She sat in a chair and watched the stars burn, lonely fires in the black sky.

She did not sleep.

11

The Best-Laid Plans of
Mice and Guys . . .

Man, it felt good to be back.

Dawn was just breaking, and the boardwalk was still bathed in shadow, but you could feel the heat already. Seth took off his Nikes, carefully balled his socks inside, and started across the sand. At the edge of the water he let the foam swirl around his toes. His jeans got wet, but what the hell. He was on spring break now. Officially.

Out across the sparkling water, somewhere in one of those incredible yachts, Summer was sleeping. The thought gave his heart a nice, electric jolt. Diana, too. That particular thought gave his heart another, less pleasant, jolt.

He wanted to go wake Summer right away, maybe even crawl into bed next to her and make out for a couple of days—as if that was going to happen in his lifetime—but it was way too early. He couldn't wait to see her face. He was arriving a whole day early, which meant a whole extra day together—a whole extra day soaking up one hundred percent Florida rays.

He started across the beach, heading nowhere in particular. A couple of eager beach stand operators were already setting up shop, lining up yellow striped umbrellas and beach chairs for rent. A beach photographer was loading film into a Polaroid camera. Down near the marina, two well-tanned, well-built girls were readying a handful of Jet Skis for rent. Already the scent of fries and suntan oil was in the air.

Up ahead on the sand, in the long shadows of high-rise condos, a big raised wooden platform was being assembled by a work crew. Judging by the MTV caps and the huge array of football-field lighting, they were going to do some filming. A big sign on the ground read MTV Spring Fling.

Seth made his way toward the marina. He checked his watch, then remembered it had no hands. He shook his head, grinning, and pulled out the backup watch in his jeans pocket. Way too early still. Summer would kill him.

He crossed to the marina and made his way past rows of glistening sailboats, bobbing gently like very expensive corks. Maybe he could rent a sunfish or a Hobie Cat and take Summer out on one. She'd love sailing. She'd been a natural at scuba diving the summer before.

Of course, he thought with a pang of regret, they couldn't really recapture what they'd had that summer. Summer was wrong about that. It would be different that week, and different that coming summer. Things had changed, and they couldn't go back once they had.

He paused to admire a sailboat, a sleek fifty-footer. Yes, it would be great to take Summer out for some sailing. Diana could go, too, he supposed. She probably had a couple of guys lined up for spring break already. Diana was like that, although she claimed she scared off males. Maybe it was true. She'd always scared him a little, with her dark, intense beauty.

Things came back to him unbidden, images he didn't want to recall. He swallowed hard. He could taste the salt in the air.

He'd passed a flower vendor just setting up shop a couple of blocks back. Maybe he'd go back, kill some time. Buy Summer some flowers, something extravagant he couldn't really afford.

He could get something for Diana, too, if he was careful. Just a polite, friendly flower, one of those puffy things the girls wore to football games. Something neutral. That would be good. That would set the right tone for this week.

He'd go buy the flowers, kill a few more minutes. Then he'd surprise Summer. He couldn't wait to see her face.

Marquez mixed a little cadmium red light with a dab of rose madder on her palette. She rolled the matchstick blind a little higher, careful not to wake Diver.

She'd never painted a sunrise before. It was such a cliché. But that morning the sun was turning the sky an intense, not-to-be-believed shade of red, sort of ripe mango meets raspberry meets banana. She was hungry, but first she wanted to capture that color.

She smeared on more and more, mixing in a frenzy, bouncing to the tune playing full-blast in her head. She'd tossed her tackle box, the one she used to hold her art stuff, into the trash before her Great Escape the day before, but at the last minute, in a moment of remorse, she'd rescued it from Hefty-bag hell. She'd thrown it in the backseat instead, not knowing why. Now she was glad she'd brought it along.

Diver stirred. He was lying on his side on a straw mat. (Gentleman that he was, he'd loaned her the sleeping bag.) His tanned arms clutched at a twisted white sheet. His mouth was open just slightly. He appeared to be smiling. It would be nice to think he was dreaming about her, but she wasn't a moron.

She shook off the memory of the previous night's excesses. So she'd come on to him, so she'd cried about J.T. It wasn't the first time on either count. And so what? One thing she'd learned a long time ago was that being embarrassed about things you'd already done was a big waste of time.

She studied Diver's hand against the sheet. It would make a nice picture, the tapering lines of his fingers, the creases in the sheet. She started mixing some raw umber and burnt sienna to get the brown of his skin. The sunrise could wait.

Diver shifted a little. "Darn," Marquez muttered under her breath. "Don't move yet."

"Huh?" Diver rolled over and smiled. "Oh. Hi, Marquez."

"Go back to the way you were. I'm capturing you for posterity."

"Cool. You seem better."

"I am better, a little. I don't know why. But I went, like, five whole minutes this morning without thinking about J.T." She sighed. "Of course, I went for an hour after that plotting revenge. Check out the sunrise, only don't move, okay?"

"I know about the sunrise." Diver gave a satisfied smile. "Why do you think I like it here?"

Marquez reached for her pad. "I think you like it here," she said in that singsong voice she always got when she was trying to talk and paint at the same time, "for the same reason I already like it. No problems, no demands, no letters telling you your SATs don't cut it. And no J.T."

"You'll get over J.T."

"Oh? And what makes you so sure?"

Diver shrugged. "You will, that's all."

To her annoyance, Diver rolled over. The sun shone on his smooth chest. He put one arm behind his head and stared at her thoughtfully. "You oughta go to art school, you know."

"You know where artists end up, most of them? Doing caricatures of fat tourists on the boardwalk." She reached for her pad again. "This time *really* don't move. The thing is, I have obligations, Diver, big ones."

"What kind of obligations?"

"Family stuff." She saw him grimace. "Not like yours. Different. I mean, my dad was imprisoned in Cuba for three years for complaining about the government. When we escaped to the U.S. in a rowboat I was just a little bitty kid, but I can remember sensing how scared my mom and dad were. We had no money, just the clothes on our backs. None of us spoke a word of English." She paused, staring out at the water that had once seemed so treacherous. "Now my dad's gas station business is in trouble, and we have to sell the house. I feel like I owe it to my family to really make something of myself, you know?"

"You can't fight your destiny."

Marquez groaned. "You and everybody else are so sure what my destiny is. How come I don't know it?"

"Because you're the most stubborn girl I've ever met, with the possible exception of my sister."

Marquez picked up a hunk of paint and flung it at Diver. It landed with a plop a couple of inches from his belly button.

Diver laughed. "You know, it kind of looks like a dolphin."

"It will when I'm done with it," Marquez said. She loaded up her brush and got down on her stomach next to Diver. "Whatever you do, don't move. I am an artist, and I will not be denied." She moved the brush in tiny flicks. "Would you settle for a whale? Kind of a Shamu thing?"

"That tickles."

"All great art comes at a price. Please stop breathing."

Diver lay very still while Marquez continued her work. "I had a dream last night, about you," he said.

Marquez looked up in surprise. All right. There really was a God.

"And Summer and Diana, and I think both my moms were in it," Diver continued. "And a guinea pig I had when I was little."

There really was a God, and She had a lousy sense of humor.

119

"I kept trying to talk to Summer," Diver continued in a faraway voice, "but every time I called her she hung up. Diana was like the operator."

Marquez finished Shamu's tail. "And where was I?"

Diver smiled. "You were just . . . I don't know. There."

"Figures." She reached for some more paint. "You know what the phone means, of course. You want to make contact with Summer."

"No. No, I don't. I can't be what she wants me to be."

"She loves you, Diver. However you are."

"You weren't there, in Minnesota. You don't know." His voice caught. "I just didn't belong there."

"But you belong here, playing pelican doctor?"

A slow smile dawned. "Yeah. Actually."

She smiled back. "Yeah, I suppose maybe you do. But how do you know that? How do you know which you is you?"

Diver considered. "I guess it's not so much that I know what's right for me as much as I know what's wrong. And that's something, anyway. It's a start."

Marquez nodded. "I feel right being here. Or less wrong, anyway. Is that okay? For a little while?"

"You have to help me feed the pelicans."

Marquez groaned. "Suddenly it feels less right." She sat up. "What do you think?"

Diver examined her work. "Cool. I may never shower again."

"One more thing." Marquez made a flourish with her brush.

"What was that?"

"My signature." She smiled. "That belly button may be worth a fortune someday." She shrugged. "Then again, maybe not."

12

Oh, What a Tangled Web She Weaves

*B*reakfast is served." Summer placed a tray on the nightstand next to Austin's bed.

Austin stared at her, blinking, then at the pink sleeve of the robe he was wearing. He sat up and ran his fingers through his tousled hair. "It's all coming back to me. You saved my life."

"Well, that's a little melodramatic, but yes."

"And then you made me wear this ridiculous robe."

"Also true. You feeling better?"

"Seeing you, I am." He reached for her hand. "I don't suppose you spent the night in here and I'm suffering from temporary amnesia?"

"Sorry."

"I had a feeling I wouldn't forget something that memorable." Austin smiled. "Thanks for listening to me ramble on last night. I felt better talking about it."

"After breakfast I'll go over to the hospital with you."

A shadow fell over Austin's face. "I guess I can't put it off forever."

"Summer?" someone called from the upper deck.

Summer frowned. "I wonder who—" She was interrupted by a soft knock on the cabin door.

"Summer? It's me!"

She gulped. "Oh, my God."

"What? Who is that?" Austin asked.

"It's Seth," Summer muttered.

"Seth, the boyfriend?" Austin asked.

Seth knocked a little harder. "Surprise!"

Summer stared back at the door, frozen in disbelief.

"I'll get it," Austin said gallantly, climbing out of bed.

"No, no, no!" Summer hissed in a loud whisper. "Seth," she called, "just a minute. I'm not decent."

"So what?" Seth said.

"Lusty lad, isn't he?" Austin offered.

"Austin, you have to hide!" Summer whispered.

Austin calmly stroked his bearded chin. He looked even more disreputable than he had yesterday.

"Out the porthole!" Summer urged. "No,

you're too big! Under the bed! No, there's not enough room under there!" She wrung her hands, pacing frantically.

"Summer, are you okay?" Seth called.

"The shower!" Summer cried. "Hide in the shower!"

"Whatever you say, but I'd really hoped to meet the boy," Austin said, shaking his head. "We have so much in common, what with our both being infatuated with you."

Summer shooed him into the bathroom, then ran to the cabin door and threw it open.

Seth pressed a paper cone full of roses into her hands. He kissed her passionately. After a few moments she pulled away and sniffed the roses. "I can't believe you're here!"

Seth stepped into the room and let out a whistle. "It's so . . . pink." He settled into an overstuffed chair. Summer gasped. He was sitting on top of Austin's wet cutoffs.

Seth grimaced, sat up, and held them up between two fingers. "Whose are these?"

"Those are mine," Summer said quickly, yanking them away. "Diana and I went in the Jacuzzi last night."

"But they're huge."

"Oh, you know. The hot water. They stretched." She rushed over, sat in his lap, and wrapped her arms around him. "Thank you for the flowers."

125

"There's a carnation in there. It's for Diana."

"You are *so* sweet. Let's go wake her up, okay?"

"Why?" he asked, incredulous.

"To give her the flower."

"I don't want to see Diana." He kissed her neck. "I want to see you. This is the official beginning of our spring break, you know."

"How did you get here early, anyway?"

"My aunt actually eloped at the last minute, can you believe it? So I hung out all evening at the airport and caught a standby."

"You are so sweet." Summer cast a nervous glance at the bathroom. "The flowers, and coming early, and Diana told me how you called about me—"

Seth gasped. "She told you?"

"Don't be silly. I thought it was cute, checking to make sure she had my flight right and all."

"Oh. Yeah." Seth pushed her aside, clearing his throat. "Look, I've been wandering the boardwalk for the past hour. Where's the head?"

"The head? Oh, you were being nautical. *That* head, the bathroom head," Summer babbled. Oh, you mean the bathroom where I'm hiding the guy who's wearing nothing but a bathrobe and a salacious grin? *That* bathroom?

She ran to the door and pointed down the hall. "It's the one with the gold plaque. Down those wooden stairs."

126

"What's that?" Seth asked, pointing.

"That?"

"That room. Isn't that a head?"

"Uh, that's, uh, out of order."

"What's wrong with it? Maybe I can fix it later."

Never tell a former handyman anything is broken. Never, ever, ever.

Just as Seth put his hand on the brass doorknob, Summer ran to him and threw her arms around him again. "Try the water bed first," she urged.

Seth grinned. "Hold that thought." He started to open the door.

"No!" Summer cried.

Just then the noise of the shower met their ears.

Seth slammed the door shut. "There's someone *in* there? Why did you tell me it was out of order?"

"Well, the toilet's out of order, but the shower's working."

Seth put his hands on his hips. "*Who* exactly is in there?"

Summer opened her mouth, waiting to see if a plausible lie might develop there. But just then the cabin door flew open and Diana appeared. She was dressed in full yacht regalia—pink robe, pink fluffy slippers, pink coffee mug.

"Seth!" she cried. "You're here early!" She gave him a quick, rather awkward hug. "What a surprise, huh, Summer?"

"Definite surprise."

"And you brought Summer roses. How sweet."

"There's a carnation in there, too. For you," Seth said in a strangely stiff voice.

"You are so thoughtful." Diana brushed past them both to the bathroom door.

"Diana, I wouldn't—"

"Oh, Summer, don't be so Midwestern," Diana chided. She winked at Seth. "It's not like I haven't seen Austin in his altogether before. You forget we used the Jacuzzi last night."

"Wait a minute." Seth's brow was furrowed. "Who the heck is Austin?" He shook a finger at Summer. "You were in a Jacuzzi last night with a naked guy?"

Diana's eyes darted to Summer's. "Please, Seth, don't go all postal on us. *I* was in the Jacuzzi with Austin. Summer and I were in it earlier, okay?"

"You were in a Jacuzzi with a naked guy?"

"He lost his bathing suit."

Seth glanced over at the wet cutoffs. He was putting two and two together, and he was very good at addition. Summer swallowed.

"Who's this Austin character, anyway?" Seth demanded of Diana. It was almost as if he'd forgotten Summer.

"Seth, I'm eighteen and unencumbered," Diana said tartly. "You're the one who's practically engaged. Now," she said, pulling open the door, "if you'll excuse me."

"Why is he in Summer's bathroom?" Seth asked doubtfully.

"The main one's not working."

"So this toilet doesn't work and that shower doesn't work?"

"No, there's nothing wrong with this toilet," Diana said.

"Yeah, Diana," Summer said pointedly. "Remember how I told you it flushes real slow?"

"Oh, that," Diana said smoothly. She gave Seth a little pat on the shoulder. "Maybe later you could put those handyman skills of yours to good use, Seth. Meantime," she said with a sly grin, "I'm going to put Austin's skills to good use."

She slipped into the bathroom and closed the door.

Summer dropped onto the water bed. She was feeling a little seasick, and this time it wasn't the yacht.

A moment later they heard a startled male shout.

Seth shook his head. "So how long's she been seeing this Austin guy?"

"Oh, not very long," Summer said in a high-pitched voice. "Not long at all."

"Well, I guess I'll go track down that other bath—"

The door flew open, and Austin and Diana

emerged. Diana had her arm around Austin's waist. Austin's hair was wet. They were both wearing pink robes. They were both smiling way too hard.

"Austin Reed." Austin extended his hand.

"Seth Warner," Seth said, taking it a little warily.

"Thanks for lending me your shower, Summer," Austin said cheerfully.

"Anytime." Summer stared at the mural on the ceiling. The woman with the tiny waist seemed to be winking at her.

"You've got yourself quite a girl there, Seth," Austin said.

Diana swatted Austin on the rear. "Hey, what am I to you?"

Austin leaned down and planted a swift but very definite kiss on Diana's lips. "You, my dear, are about to make me some coffee."

"Meet you upstairs," Diana called, leading Austin toward the door.

Austin paused in the doorway. "Isn't this great? Spring break on a yacht." He grinned at Summer. "I think we're all going to get to know each other very well."

"Two over easy with sausage, two sunny-side up with raisin toast, two scrambled with bacon, and one glass of water with Alka-Seltzer."

The waitress set down the hot plates, then

handed Summer her water with a sneer. "You spring break kids never learn, do you? Every year it's the same. Tear this town to shreds and puke all over the beach and tip the decent, hardworking locals like crap." She sighed as she left. "Oh, to be young again."

"You feel okay?" Seth asked, draping his arm around her shoulders protectively.

Summer watched the tablets fizz. "I'm just not very hungry, is all."

"She didn't get much sleep last night," Austin said.

Seth raised an eyebrow.

Austin shrugged innocently. "She and Diana were up till all hours. There was a great deal of unnecessary giggling."

"We had a lot to catch up on," Diana said, sipping her grapefruit juice. "Gossip, girl talk . . . secrets."

At Diana's suggestion, they'd walked from the yacht over to the beachside Denny's. Summer would have preferred a few minutes to collect her thoughts, to take Austin aside and explain that now that Seth was here it would be a good idea for Austin to move on. But there hadn't been any time for that. And besides, she could hardly just abandon him after saving his life the night before. And after promising to go to the hospital with him that day.

"Better eat up," Austin advised. Despite what

had happened the previous night, he was acting awfully perky, playing up his role as Diana's new boyfriend. "We've got a big day ahead of us. Vegging out on the beach can be so tiring."

"The beach—" Summer began.

"I thought we'd make a day of it," Austin said. "The four of us. Maybe get some volleyball action going, rent some Jet Skis later."

Summer could barely control her reaction. Seth was looking annoyed, and even Diana seemed a little put off. "I thought . . ." Summer hesitated. "Weren't you talking about something you had to do today, Austin? I thought I heard you talking to Diana about it. Something about your dad?"

"That's this afternoon. This morning there's plenty of time for hanging out. Seth, my man, you into volleyball?"

Seth poked at his eggs. "Yeah, sure, whatever."

"Austin, they probably want a little time together," Diana said helpfully.

"Oh," Austin said, as if the thought had never occurred to him. "Well, sure they do. But there's plenty of time for that, right, Seth?"

"Diana," Summer said suddenly, "I've got an idea. Let's go call Marquez's house."

"My eggs will get cold." Diana paused, catching Summer's glare. "Actually, they're kind of runny, anyway."

"Don't you have that cell phone of yours?" Seth asked. "Over Christmas you carried it around like it was the Hope diamond or something."

At the mention of Christmas Diana's face clouded for a moment. "No, I left it on the yacht," she said. "And don't spit on technology, Seth. That cell phone is my link to civilization. With the touch of a button you can speed-dial Takeout Taxi and Neiman-Marcus."

Summer led the way through the crowded restaurant to a pay phone by the rest rooms. Two blond high school girls were using it, passing the receiver back and forth.

"Diana, what am I going to do?" Summer groaned. "I don't want Seth to get the wrong idea, but I think Austin is kind of messed up and needs me right now."

"That would explain why you had two guys fighting over your heart-shaped water bed this morning," Diana said, just loud enough to be sure the girls using the phone would overhear.

Summer shot her a dirty look. "This is so awful. Do you think Seth suspects? He's acting kind of weird."

"Does he have anything to suspect?"

"No! I just wanted to help Austin." Summer groaned again. "This is getting out of hand. I wanted this to be the perfect romantic spring break."

"Generally it's a good idea not to bring along an extra guy in that case."

Summer punched her in the arm. The blond girls hung up the phone, but they lingered nearby, obviously eavesdropping.

"Hey, I rescued you in the name of preserving your relationship with Seth," Diana protested. "I'm the one who had to walk in on Austin showering."

"You're a brave woman, Diana."

"I do what I can. And now I'm stuck playing girlfriend to a perfect stranger. Not that I mind the leading man. He's got kind of a brooding, lost-soul thing going for him, sort of Kurt Cobainesque."

"Don't say that." Summer winced.

"What?"

"Don't bring up famous dead rock stars. Austin sort of tried to kill himself last night."

Diana's eyes widened. She touched Summer's shoulder. "Are you sure?"

Summer nodded. She knew Diana had had her own dark experience flirting with suicide the past summer. "He swam out really far. I caught up with him. By the way, I think I tied the dinghy up wrong." She rubbed her eyes.

Diana thought for a moment. "The question is, why's Austin going along with this game?"

"I haven't had a chance to talk to him since Seth got here, so I have no idea. Unless he'd rather hang around this soap opera than deal with—" Summer caught herself. Austin's problems were his own. She didn't feel right telling Diana what he'd revealed during the night.

Diana patted her on the arm. "Look, I'm willing to play along for a while. I want this week to be perfect for you and Seth. Totally."

"You're a good friend, Diana."

"I'm a good cousin," Diana corrected. "And it's not like I have a choice. I have to keep seeing you on holidays and at family reunions." She reached into her purse. "Now, let's try calling Marquez's mom."

"Then what?"

"Then we go back to the table, you drink your Alka-Seltzer, and we head to the beach and cross our fingers."

Diana pointed to the phone. The blond girls were still watching them. "You done?" Diana asked one of them.

"Oh. Yeah. Absolutely." She grabbed her friend. "Why can't we have a spring break like theirs?" she muttered as they headed off. "Some girls have all the luck."

13

Three's a Crowd, Four's a Complete Disaster

Summer lay on her very large, very pink beach towel and tried to fall asleep. It was the perfect beach day. Not too hot. A nice breeze. The usual beach stuff, the stuff she'd dreamed about for months, surrounded her. Wall-to-wall humanity for plenty of people-watching. Coconut-scented air. Sand like powdered sugar. A sky almost too blue.

Overhead a small plane flew back and forth, advertising Bain de Soleil and MTV Spring Fling on a long white banner. Jet Skis buzzed on the bay like giant mosquitos. Voices rose and fell in a hypnotic lull, interrupted occasionally by the sharp trill of a lifeguard's whistle.

Seth and Austin lay on either side of her. Diana lay next to Austin. Their bodies glimmered with suntan lotion. Their eyes were closed. Everyone seemed perfectly content, except Summer.

It was the perfect spring break day, except it was not quite as she'd imagined it. For one thing, Marquez was missing. For another, Austin had not exactly been part of the plan.

"I wish Marquez were here," Summer said to no one in particular. She sat up and checked for a tan line. She'd slopped on too much SPF 15. No one would even be able to tell she'd been to Florida.

"Mmm-hmm," Diana murmured sleepily. "At least we know she's okay."

"We know she left a message on her parents' machine this morning saying she was bird-watching with a good friend," Summer reminded her. "That is not the same as being okay."

"How do you know?" Seth asked, lazily rolling onto his side.

"Since when is Marquez into birds? And who's the friend? We're her friends, Diana and me."

"Could be someone we don't know," Diana pointed out. "A guy, even."

Seth was smiling at Summer. "Nice suit."

"You've already seen this one."

"That was in Dayton's under fluorescent lights. Now you're in natural lighting." He leaned across his towel and kissed her lightly. "Can you believe we're really here?"

Just as she opened her mouth to answer,

someone nudged Summer from the other side. Austin was holding her bottle of suntan lotion. "Would you mind doing my back?"

"Why don't you ask Diana, Austin?" she said pointedly.

"She's sleeping."

"She's just dozing."

"No, she's not," Diana said in a slurred voice. "She's definitely sleeping."

Austin held out the bottle.

"Oh, all right," Summer muttered, but before she could take the bottle, Seth reached over her and grabbed it from Austin. He took aim and squirted a messy glob of suntan lotion on Austin's back. "There," he said grouchily. "That should hold you."

Austin grinned. "Thanks, Seth," he said, obviously enjoying his annoyance. "I have such delicate skin."

Summer sent him a warning stare. She needed to get him alone somewhere so they could talk, and soon.

"So," Austin said, apparently oblivious to her stares, "are we all on for the big MTV thing tonight?"

"Austin, hon," Diana piped up, "you and I need some quality time alone, don't you think?"

"Well, sure," he said, looking a little lost, "but I just thought we could all, you know . . . do

139

quality time together." He gazed at Summer longingly. "He's right. It is a nice suit."

Diana swatted Austin. "Hey, what about mine?"

"Also a nice suit," Austin said, eyes glued to Summer.

Seth grimaced. "Speaking of suits, I thought Diana said you didn't have one."

"These are cutoffs."

"So they are," Seth said, casting Summer a sidelong look. He jumped up abruptly. "I'm going in." He held out a hand to Summer. "Coming?"

"Um, you go ahead. I'm kind of not up for it."

"Come on, Summer. Lake Calhoun has been frozen since November. This is the ocean, and we're in Florida. This is what we've been fantasizing about for months."

"Actually, you go out far enough, it gets pretty cold," Austin said wryly.

"Later," Summer promised. "Diana, how about you?"

"Mmm," she murmured.

Summer tossed a handful of sand onto her cousin's back. "How about now?" she said meaningfully, casting a quick glance at Austin.

"Oh. Now. Sure." Diana sat up quickly. "Especially now that I have sand superglued to my back." She nodded to Seth. "It's only been twenty minutes since we ate, Seth. You sure you want to risk it?"

"Shut up, Diana," Seth said, with more than a trace of annoyance. He ran out into the ocean and dove beneath a wave.

"Such a wild man," Diana said. She set aside her sunglasses and headed, in her usual graceful, regal fashion, toward the water, garnering plenty of approving glances as she walked.

"She's quite a girl," Austin said.

"Yes, you two make a lovely couple," Summer said. "But Austin, this game has got to stop."

"Game?" He brushed sand off her shoulder.

"I want to help you. I want to be your friend. I'll go see your dad with you this afternoon, and we'll figure out something to tell Seth."

"Not necessary." Austin lay on his side. "I called the hospital from Denny's. He's in pretty bad shape today. The nurse said to try again tomorrow, because he'll be sleeping most of the day today. He's heavily drugged, I take it." His voice was calm, almost matter-of-fact.

"So you're going tomorrow, then?"

"I don't know. Maybe," he snapped. "I'm not in any hurry, okay?"

"But I'm sure he'll want to see you—"

"Don't be so sure. There's a good chance he won't even know who I am, Summer."

She fell silent. "I didn't know it was that bad," she said.

"It's bad." He forced a smile. "So anyway, I

thought that for today, at least, I'd just hang out with you and Seth and Diana, my girlfriend, if that's okay. That is her name, right?"

"It's not okay," Summer said adamantly, so loudly people on a nearby blanket turned to stare. She took a deep breath. "It's not okay," Summer said more quietly, "because this isn't what I'd planned, Austin. This is supposed to be a nice, relaxing spring break for me and Seth. And if you stay, I have the feeling it's going to be anything but relaxing."

"This isn't what I'd planned on, either, Summer," Austin said, and suddenly he was completely serious. He eased his hand across her towel until their fingers touched. Summer checked the shore. Out in the ocean, Seth and Diana were treading water, side by side. "But last night I realized that—and this is not just because you happened to save my life, although that certainly earned you valuable bonus points—I'm in distinct danger of falling in love with you."

Summer pulled her hand away. She sat up stiffly on her towel, carefully occupying herself with burying her feet in the sand. She fervently wished she could bury her whole self.

"You shouldn't say stuff like that, Austin," she said at last. "To begin with, you don't know me at all, not really."

"I know enough. I know you're the kind of girl who'd run into a men's room and toss my life's work in a toilet. I know you're the kind of girl who'd risk her own life to go charging out into the middle of the Atlantic and save someone's life." His voice fell. "I know you're the kind of girl who'd kiss a guy on the Skyway to Tomorrowland like he'd never been kissed before."

She looked away. For some annoying reason, her eyes were hot with tears. She was glad for the safety of her sunglasses.

"You can't plan everything, Summer," Austin said. "Sometimes you just have to wait and see what happens."

"I know what's going to happen. I am going to go with you to the hospital, and then I am going to go to the dance tonight with Seth, and then . . ." She hesitated. "And then you and I will say good-bye, and Seth and I will fly back north, and maybe someday I'll buy a book of your poems."

Austin rolled onto his stomach. "Do me a favor while you're telling me to get lost, okay? Rub in that glop."

Summer checked the water again. Seth and Diana were farther down the beach, closer to shore, still swimming together. "Okay, but it doesn't mean anything. I'm just trying to provide you with adequate sun protection."

She rubbed the lotion into his warm, smooth skin. He felt different from Seth, more sinewy. She ran her fingers slowly down his backbone. "There," she said, pulling her hand away.

"You know what I realized last night, in addition to the fact that I'm falling for you? I realized you were right when you blurted that stuff about spring break out in the ocean. You were saying *carpe diem.*"

Summer lay down on her towel. "I couldn't have been saying it. I don't even know what it means."

"It means 'seize the day.' It means I have a choice. I can spend a few precious days with the most enchanting girl I've ever come across in my nineteen-plus years. Or I can spend them discovering whether I have an incurable and fatal disease." He grinned. "Call me crazy, but I'm going with option A."

"I'm not an option," Summer said gently. "I'm already in love. I really, really do love Seth."

Austin leaned over and, before she could object, brushed her lips with a kiss so gentle and fleeting it might just have been the breeze. "I know you do. I also know that you're about to realize you love me even more."

The radio was blaring Dance Hall Crashers—she'd stocked up on batteries at the Shell market—and Marquez was in high gear. She spun around Ken's van, paintbrush in one hand, diet Coke in the other. It was her masterpiece. It was better than her wall—her soon-to-be former wall—back home.

It was the pelican from hell. It was the Godzilla of pelicans. It was Peli-Kong.

Diver approached, carrying Harold wrapped in a towel.

"What do you think?" Marquez asked, making another sweep of the van.

"Incredible," Diver said. "Ken will be so excited."

"I had to paint out the old one and start from scratch," she explained. "But see how his wings kind of curve around the whole side now? It's like he's coming right at you. You know, I never really *got* pelicans before. But they're so *Flintstones,* aren't they? Like really ugly can openers." She stroked Harold's back tentatively. "How's he doing?"

"Much better. In a couple more weeks he'll be good as new." Diver grinned. "You've been painting up a storm today."

"I know. I kind of like this running away stuff. Whatever I do, it doesn't really matter, you know? I feel free of everybody."

"You aren't, not really," Diver said quietly. "They have a way of hanging around. At night, especially."

Marquez stopped gyrating and turned down the radio a little. "You miss them, don't you? Summer and your mom and dad?"

Diver stroked Harold's head. "Yeah. I miss them."

"She misses you, too. Every time I talked to her she brought you up."

"I can imagine."

"Well, the word *jerk* did come up a few billion

Katherine Applegate

times, but you have to understand, Diver. Summer's very, you know . . . she's the kind of person who doesn't give up on people. I think she felt sort of betrayed when you left. She figured she was trying, so why couldn't you?"

Diver's expression hardened. It was as close to angry as Marquez had ever seen him. "Maybe if I'm not like Summer, it's because I didn't have Summer's life. She wasn't kidnapped. She wasn't . . . treated badly. She didn't run away and live on the streets."

"I know that, Diver. Don't take it out on me, okay? I'm just telling you what I think Summer's feeling. I'm not saying she's right or wrong. Don't forget, I'm hiding out with you here. I'm not exactly dealing with stuff either." She paused to touch up a spot on her giant pelican's right eye. "I'm on your side."

Diver nodded. "I know. It's just that you're only passing through, Marquez. I'm not."

"Who knows? Maybe I'll stay here forever with you, customizing vans with bird portraits. I'm sure there's a market. We'll grow old together, you and me and Ken and Harold."

Diver laughed, but just a little. "You're not really hiding out. You called your mom today. You'll be gone soon."

Marquez put her arm around Diver. "I have an idea. There was this ad on the radio a while ago. Some big MTV thing tonight downtown in

Boca Beach, right on the water. Let's go. We'll lose ourselves in the sweaty crowd and drown our sorrows in diet Coke. I've had enough beer for one lifetime. What do you say?"

"I don't know."

"It'll be fun. I won't even make you dance if you don't want to."

Diver relented a little. "I liked dancing with you."

"Me, too." Kissing you, too, she added silently. Even if you didn't kiss me back.

"So it's a deal?" Marquez said.

"Sure." Diver turned to go. "I gotta put Harold back."

She watched him walk away. He was so like Summer in some ways, same golden hair, same sweetness, same habit of thinking way, way too much. It occurred to her that it was remotely possible Summer and Diana might be at the MTV thing that night. But that seemed really unlikely. Diana was too antisocial, and they would undoubtedly be hanging out on the Love Boat, wherever it was docked. Besides, Boca was a big town. There was no way they'd run into them.

Too bad. She was already kind of missing them a little bit. And it wouldn't entirely be a bad thing for Diver and Summer to reconnect.

But he didn't want to, and Marquez was cool with that. She understood. She liked it there, too.

It sure beat the real world.

14

Not-So-Dirty Dancing

"Wanna dance, babe?"

Diana glanced at the obviously drunken frat boy in the University of Illinois T-shirt. He was cute, in a hairy-knuckled, preverbal sort of way.

"I'm looking for someone. Sorry," she said, brushing past him and weaving her way deeper into the crowd.

Looking for someone. That was about right. She'd never seen so many bodies pressed together in one space before, and yet she felt strangely alone. She didn't have to be, of course. It would be easy enough to meet guys. Everyone was there with the express intent of pairing up. And she'd gotten plenty of attention. She was wearing a new red bathing suit, cut high in the thighs and with a low scoop neck. Her dark hair was down, flowing loose around her shoulders.

She paused near a lifeguard stand. A couple was dancing on the chair, hoping for just a moment of camera time. But then, everybody seemed to hoping for their fifteen minutes of fame. Since sundown the entire beach had been mobbed with spring breakers there for the MTV filming. Huge black speakers vibrated the air with music, so loud the sand seemed to throb. Strobe lights and searchlights flashed the area like heat lightning. Camera operators on large cranes hovered over the gathering, swooping in to catch the best dancers and the best bodies, with an emphasis on the latter.

Someone tapped Diana on the shoulder. "I said no—" she began.

"Whoa." Seth laughed good-naturedly. "You on auto-reject?"

"Sorry," Diana said as the pressure of bodies pushed her close to him. She had to yell to make herself heard. "It's that kind of night. Where's Summer?"

"She went back to the yacht to get a sweater." Seth leaned close to be heard. "Where's Austin?"

"He's . . . around someplace." Back at the yacht, probably, though there was no point in telling Seth that. The truth was, Diana was getting tired of the Austin game. He obviously was madly in love with Summer, even if Summer couldn't tell. He'd mooned around her all day. And there was something kind of demoralizing about pretending you were hot for someone who wasn't even bothering to pretend he was hot for you.

"Dance?" Seth asked, nearly screaming.

Diana nodded her answer. They were sucked into the seething crowd. "Genocide," by the Offspring. Good. Diana felt like cutting loose a little. The strobes flashed and the searchlights panned, revealing other people in disjointed bits and pieces—a mouth wide open in laughter, a pair of flailing arms, a face with eyes closed, lost to the throbbing music.

For a moment Seth was illuminated by the intense white light. He was so perfect for Summer. The sweet, all-American, prom king, football player type. A genuine nice guy.

Well, more or less.

"What?" he screamed.

Diana realized she was staring at him. "Nothing. I was just thinking how good you are for Summer."

"What's a bummer?"

Diana shook her head, pointing to her ears. She took Seth by the arm and pulled him toward the edge of the crowd. It was like fighting a riptide, but after several minutes they were on the periphery. There, closer to the marina, the music was still loud, but conversation was actually possible. There was more room to dance or to make out, and people were making the most of both opportunities. The lights were sucked up in the vast darkness of the overcast night. The moon was just a possibility, lingering behind thick clouds.

They made their way past two couples in hot embrace on the sand. The music slowed to something more mellow. Mariah Carey. Diana didn't recognize the song.

Seth was scanning the waterfront. "I'm afraid Summer won't find us."

"Sure she will. We're probably easier to spot out here. So. Dance?"

Even in the darkness, she could tell he was uncomfortable. "We were just dancing a second ago," she pointed out.

"This is a slow dance." He swallowed. "I don't want Summer to think—"

"To think what? That you had a chaste, platonic, meaningless dance with her dateless cousin?"

Seth laughed a little. "You're dateless by choice, Diana. You know you could have anybody here."

"Except you," she said, instantly regretting it.

She laughed lightly to show Seth she didn't mean anything by it and held out her hands. Seth took them in his, glancing over his shoulder. She put her arms around his waist and they were, despite Seth's obvious reluctance, finally dancing, each one careful not to let their bodies touch more than was absolutely necessary.

"Diana?" Seth said. "Is there anything . . . has anything been going on I should know about?"

"What do you mean?" she asked.

"Summer. It's just been sort of weird today."

"Welcome to spring break. I told her and Marquez it would probably be this way. Everybody has such expectations. All this artificial fun gets to you after a while. Of course, this is right up Marquez's alley. She loves the vulgar and tasteless."

He wasn't smiling. "That's not what I meant. I don't know what I meant. It's probably just jet lag."

"Seth, you can't get jet lag moving from Central Standard Time to Eastern."

He draped his hands around her shoulders, and she felt a wonderful, terrible ache of longing that she definitely did not want to be feeling. It wasn't fair. Summer was fending off Austin's advances while Seth remained hopelessly in love with her, and Diana was left feeling . . . what? What *was* it she was feeling for Seth?

That night at New Year's when they'd been stuck in the snowdrift waiting for a tow, was that what she really felt for Seth? It had started out so innocently, just a what-the-heck New Year's kiss at midnight, two old friends stuck in a funny situation they knew they'd laugh about later. But after they'd pulled away, Seth had looked at her in a different way, and when he'd reached for her again and they kissed, it hadn't been two old friends. It had been like nothing Diana had ever felt before, not with any of the guys she'd dated.

It had been the kind of kiss where you lost yourself, the kind that was almost scary because you weren't sure you'd ever find yourself again if you let it go on too long.

Of course, she'd told herself, it was just the illicit nature of it all. A stolen kiss. They were being bad, sneaking around behind sweet Summer's back, and wasn't it kind of fun, like that first time you skipped school? She'd told herself that Seth had always just been a buddy, a guy she'd never looked at that way. She'd told herself that she was just feeling lost and adrift, that her mom was off on tour and she was stuck with relatives over the holidays. And that maybe she was a little jealous of Summer and Seth, so much the perfect happy couple.

But of course she'd been lying to herself about all those things.

"So you think everything's okay?" Seth asked.

Was he holding her a little closer deliberately? Could it be he was so totally into Summer that he wasn't even aware of the way his body was grazing Diana's? Wasn't he feeling the same electricity when they touched this way?

"Everything's fine, Seth. You worry too

much. I can't believe you called me yesterday just to tell me not to mention the obviously unmentionable."

He stopped dancing. His grip on her shoulders was tight. "You promise you didn't tell her about what happened between us?"

It wasn't as if she hadn't thought about it. "Give me a break. Summer's my cousin. She and Marquez are my . . . my best friends."

The irony cut at her. Her best friends. One of whom had run away from home, and Diana didn't have a clue where or why. And one whose boyfriend Diana had just happened to grope as a sort of belated Christmas present to herself.

She dropped her head on Seth's shoulder, and they started dancing again. He seemed more relaxed now.

Diana could still tell Summer what had happened. It would send Summer running to Austin, who was conveniently located on the yacht, thanks to Diana. Then Diana would have Seth all to herself.

She could still do it. It wasn't as though she hadn't stolen other girls' boyfriends.

It made it so much more difficult when you happened to really like the other girl.

"There you are! I've been looking all over the place!" Summer was charging along the beach, with Austin in tow.

Austin wagged a finger at Diana. "Naughty,

naughty," he said. "I leave you for five minutes, and here you are with another guy."

Diana broke free of Seth. "He's not another guy," she said, grabbing Austin's hand with a sigh. "He's my cousin's boyfriend."

Summer swung Seth's hand lightly as they walked along the beach. The surf was cold between her toes, a too-familiar reminder of her lifesaving effort the night before.

"Finally," she said, "I have you all to myself."

Seth paused. He pulled her close and kissed her, sweetly and almost reverently, on the lips. "My thoughts exactly."

"The rest of our time should be better," Summer said. "I get the feeling Austin's leaving tomorrow."

"Diana didn't mention anything about it."

Summer shrugged. "He was on the yacht. He happened to say he couldn't stay the whole time."

The truth was, he'd followed her to the yacht, where Summer had told him in no uncertain terms that he had to leave. They were the same no uncertain terms she'd used earlier that day, but this time they'd seemed to penetrate. She'd told him she would go with him to see his dad at the hospital the next day, but that was it. He was going to have to move on.

She was feeling liberated now, more relaxed at

long last. This was the moment that had sustained her through frigid minus-thirty-degree days in January. She was with Seth, in love, on a beautiful beach, Austin was leaving, and life was good.

They sat in the cool sand and kissed for a long time. After a while, Summer couldn't help laughing.

"What?" Seth demanded, feigning indignation. "Before it was yawning. Now you're laughing. Male egos are highly fragile, you know."

"No, no," Summer protested. "I was just thinking how it's so much easier to make out without seventeen layers of sweaters and down between you."

"And don't forget the deadly stick shift problem."

She sat up, shaking sand out of her hair. "Of course, there is the sand problem. It always looks so good in the movies, but making out on the beach can get kind of gritty."

"Better gritty than frozen." Seth grinned. "By the way, do you realize you're the most beautiful girl here?"

"So it's true what they say about love being blind."

"I'm absolutely serious."

"Seth, I know you've been performing sneak ogling."

He pulled her on top of him. "And what exactly is that?"

"You know, where you undress a girl mentally and then pretend you're talking to me about the national debt or something. It's like warp-speed cheating, so fast you can't detect it with the naked eye."

Seth stopped smiling. "I would never cheat on you, Summer. Mentally or otherwise."

"All guys mentally cheat," Summer said. "It's in the guy code of ethics." She rolled off him and brushed sand off her legs. The subject of cheating was not one she was anxious to pursue.

Seth was staring out at the water pensively. "I think guys, you know, are really unsure sometimes about . . . well, I think sometimes they just want reassurance. It doesn't mean anything when they, you know, look around."

"Go ahead, try to defend your gender," Summer said lightly.

"I've known guys at school who were really in love, but they screwed around anyway, just because they could. Like it was a test or something. You know?"

He was looking at her so intently. Was he asking about Austin, trying to tell her that he knew and understood? Summer felt her stomach lurch. He'd been with Diana just now. Had Diana said something, let the story slip?

"Seth," Summer said, gathering up all her courage, "are you trying to say something?"

She waited for what seemed like an eternity. It

would be okay, she told herself. She would tell him the truth—the kissing, the poetry, the attraction, the feelings . . . yes, feelings . . . she'd had for Austin. She would tell Seth, and he would understand.

Seth stood and extended his hand. "The only thing I want to say is, when the heck do we get to try out those candles and love poems?" She joined him, and he kissed her on the tip of her nose. "Come to think of it, maybe those won't be necessary."

"Maybe not," Summer said. Especially since they're slightly used love poems now, she added silently.

Seth nodded toward the party. "Come on. I'll race you back."

He let her get a head start, then caught up until they were side by side, racing across the damp, cool sand, kicking up the surf.

Seth didn't know. He didn't know, and if she kept her mouth shut, there was no reason for him to ever know.

Austin would be gone the next day. He was a blip. An aberration.

A lie she could never, ever reveal.

The thought made her slow. She stopped, winded. The music moved through the air like a force field. The cameras were swooping, the lights crazed. People were dancing everywhere— on the yachts, on the condo balconies, on the beach, even in the water. People were even dancing on the empty lifeguard chairs.

"You wimp, I gave you a head start," Seth chided.

Summer started to answer, then stopped. She clutched Seth's arm. "Seth," she said, "that girl on the lifeguard stand."

"I am not looking, and never shall look, at any other woman unless she is fully clothed and over ninety."

Summer blinked. The girl on the chair was moving gracefully, totally engrossed in the music, oblivious to the camera swooping in to get a shot of her.

"No, really. That girl on the chair. If I didn't know better, I'd swear that was Marquez."

15

You Can Fool All of the People Some of the Time, but You Can't Fool Diana for Long

Marquez was hot. She was dancing like a maniac, which was pretty much how she always danced, except that this time there was a camera focused on her. She was only vaguely aware of the lifeguard chair beneath her feet. If she closed her eyes and just kind of let go, it was almost as if she were flying. . . .

"Marquez! *Marquez! It's us!*"

Marquez's eyes flew open. A blinding spotlight was focused on her. "Keep moving, girl," a camera operator yelled, and then she did. She took a step backward and the chair was gone, and then she really *was* flying.

She landed hard, extremely hard, right on her butt at the base of the lifeguard stand.

"Marquez! Are you all right?"

The voice was much closer, and it was Summer's, definitely Summer's. Marquez wanted to get up, but the camera operator and the guy with the spotlight had decided to zero in on her in her moment of complete and utter humiliation.

Marquez froze, torn between wanting to hide and wanting to laugh and wanting to run. Then she remembered Diver. *Run.* That was the operative word here.

The camera pulled back. Evidently she wasn't entertaining enough anymore. Marquez stood and brushed the sand off her rump. "You okay, girl?" a nearby guy asked.

And then Marquez saw them. Or at least she saw enough of Summer's blond head and Seth's dark one to know it was them, weaving through the crowd.

She had to warn Diver. She had to, but . . . she *really* wanted to see Summer.

"Over here!" Marquez called. "Summer!"

Summer finally broke through the crowd. There was much squealing and hugging and where-the-heck-have-you-been-ing, and then they ran into Diana and some extremely cute new guy named Austin, and they had to do it all over again.

Marquez herded them into one of the nearby hotel lobbies to talk. She knew Diver was out walking along the beach. He'd danced for a while, then fallen into a melancholy slump. So she figured a hotel lobby would be a good place to take Summer and the others. She didn't mind blowing her own cover, not really. But she didn't want to blow Diver's.

"We were so worried, Marquez," Summer chided.

"We were so worried and PO'ed," Diana added, arms crossed over her chest.

They settled into some leather chairs surrounded by huge potted palms. "I called my mom and told her to tell you guys I was okay," Marquez said. Even as she said it she knew how lame it sounded. Still and all, she couldn't help beaming. "It's so great to see you, Summer. You, too, Seth. You, Diana, I've seen plenty of. You, Austin"—she winked—"I wouldn't mind seeing more of."

"Don't mind Marquez," Diana said to Austin. "She's in heat again. But she's had all her shots and she's paper-trained."

"And you wonder why I ran off," Marquez said.

"Why *did* you, Marquez?" Summer asked. She looked so worried and pained that Marquez suddenly felt lousy.

"You weren't really worried, were you?" Marquez asked.

"Yes," Summer cried.

"No," Diana cried.

Marquez shrugged. "Man, I'm really sorry. I just all of a sudden couldn't take it anymore, you know? With J.T. and all, and my dad selling the place, and school—" She looked at Summer. "You know about J.T., right?"

Summer nodded. "I'm so sorry."

"He's gone. Forgotten. History. I have a new man in my life." Instantly she regretted opening her too-big mouth. "Anyway, I figured you'd all just go, 'That's Marquez, no biggie, she'll show up one of these days.'"

"It was more along the lines of 'That's Marquez, easy come easy go, can I have her CD player?'" Diana said.

Marquez groaned. "Like you couldn't buy twenty with your hourly allowance."

"Actually"—Diana leaned close and held out her hand—"I've been a little financially strapped lately. Can you guess why, Marquez?"

Marquez flashed her a grin. "Diana, Diana, my good friend Diana. Did you know you have a ten-grand limit on that card?"

"You didn't . . ."

"Puh-leeze. Only you could run up a ten-thousand-dollar tab that fast. I bought some aspirin and tampons and Chee-tos, and I made a charitable donation, okay?"

"To the Maria Marquez Foundation for Wayward Tramps, no doubt. Hand it over, you klepto."

Marquez hesitated. "It's . . . not here. It's with my purse."

"It's going to be the Maria Marquez *Memorial* Foundation if you don't cough up my card."

"It's with my stuff."

"Which is where, Marquez?" Summer asked, still obviously filled with concern. "Where have you been staying?"

"Well, it's a gold card, Summer. So only the best four-star hotels, naturally."

Summer and Seth and Austin and Diana were all looking at her. Waiting. Marquez swallowed. She was not going to rat on Diver. Even if she'd halfway hoped she'd run into Summer there, even if she'd maybe hoped Diver and Summer would reconnect by chance. She wasn't going to *make* it happen and take the rap when it didn't work out.

"I have an idea." She sprang to her feet. "I'll come see you guys in the next day or so. I'll bring the card. We'll party. How is the Love Boat, anyway?"

"It has a heart-shaped water bed," Austin offered.

"So where are you docked?"

Summer gave her directions. "But Marquez, can't you come with us now?" she pleaded. "Please. You're missing spring break. And I have lots to . . . to tell you."

Marquez saw the quick flicker of gazes from Summer to Austin to Diana. She wondered what *that* was all about.

"Look, I've gotta run," Marquez said. "Hey, did you see my MTV debut? Right on my butt, can you believe it?"

"I believe it," Diana offered with a grin. "Actually, I enjoyed it immensely."

"Marquez, wait."

Summer was grabbing her hand, making her feel trapped. Questions were coming, Marquez could feel it.

"Who's this new guy?" Summer asked. "Are you sure he's okay? You're not staying with some stranger, are you? Please tell me no."

"Trust me, Summer. He's absolutely safe. I can't even get him to kiss me."

"Imagine that," Diana said, but even she was looking at Marquez with evident worry. "Marquez," Diana said lightly, "Summer's right. Why don't you stay with us? We'll even let you have the heart-shaped water bed."

"Gotta run." Marquez was halfway to the door. "Man, it's good to see you again. Pier nineteen, right?"

"Right," Summer said. "Marquez?"

Marquez opened the door. She was almost free. "Yeah?"

"Promise this guy's okay?"

"He's the best, Summer. Really, he is. I think you'd like him if you got to know him the way I have."

*　　*　　*

166

Summer awoke the next morning to the sound of conversation and the smell of coffee. She found Seth and Diana at the dining table on the upper deck. They were both wearing bathing suits and already shimmering with suntan lotion. Austin was near the bow, staring off at the water. He had on a light blue denim shirt with the sleeves rolled up and a pair of worn jeans. It wasn't a fun-in-the-sun kind of outfit.

It looked as though they were going to the hospital after all.

The day was almost gaudy with sunlight. The whole world seemed to be ablaze. Summer had to squint as she made her way to the table.

"Hey," Seth said. "I was going to bring you breakfast in bed."

Summer kissed him. "I could go back to bed."

"Stay here." Seth pushed back his chair. "I'll go get it. Coffee and raisin toast, right?"

"Where can I get one of them?" Diana asked a little wistfully as Seth hustled off.

Summer glanced over at Austin. He acknowledged her with a brief smile, then turned back to the ocean. He'd shaved, she noticed.

"Guess what I've been doing while you were snoring away in your little love nest," Diana said. She pointed to her telephone. "I made a call to my credit card company to track down the most recent charges. Apparently Marquez has been doing her fine dining at the Shell minimarket on

167

Crescent Island. That's about thirty miles south of here. And it turns out she wasn't lying about her charitable contributions, the low-life thief. I heard about this two-hundred-and-fifty-dollar charge at a place called Peli-Ken's, so I'm thinking it's some restaurant, right?"

Summer took a steaming cup of coffee from Seth. "Thanks. Okay, so what was it?"

"I just called. Some guy who sounds like Popeye answered. Told me it's a bird hospital. You know, one of those wildlife clinics."

Summer nodded slowly, hoping the caffeine would help her make the connection Diana seemed to be expecting. "So she gave your money to a bird sanctuary? Why would Marquez do that?"

"Here's what's interesting. The Popeye guy wasn't the first person to answer the phone. The first person to answer the phone was a younger guy. When I told him what I wanted to know, all of a sudden he shut up and passed the phone to Popeye."

Summer took another sip. "Diana, I'm sorry. I'm just not tracking."

"It was a very familiar guy's voice, Summer." Diana was staring at her intently, and so was Seth. "I think it was Diver."

Summer set down her mug and closed her eyes. When she opened them, Diana was still watching her, waiting. Summer was waiting for a reaction, too, but all she felt was a kind of hollow coldness in the pit of her stomach.

"Are you sure?" she asked.

"No, not sure. But doesn't it all sort of fit together? Marquez runs off and says she's with some really nice, safe guy. And you have to admit it's just the kind of place Diver would end up in. You know how tree-huggy he is. And Marquez was always drooling over him from afar. I mean, it just fits." She tapped her manicured nails on the table. "I'll bet he was here last night. I'll bet you anything."

Summer tightened her grip on her mug. "But why would Marquez lie to me like that? She knows how upset I was about Diver's leaving Minnesota. She knows how worried my mom and dad have been. How bad everybody feels. How mad we were at him——"

She paused. Diana was nodding slowly. "Exactly," she said. "Marquez is probably trying to protect Diver. In her own distorted, bizarro-world mind, she probably thought she was protecting you, too. You know how she hates confrontations. She doesn't like other people's messes." Diana shook her head. "Just their credit cards."

"She should have told me. She shouldn't have lied. She's my friend."

"She's Diver's friend, too," Seth pointed out gently.

"Don't be so hard on her, Summer." Diana exchanged a glance with Seth. "Sometimes people do stupid things, that's all. God knows Marquez makes a habit of it. She didn't mean to hurt you."

"Why are you two defending her? I have every right to be angry. I'm angry at both of them." She pushed back her chair. "Where is this place, anyway, this pelican place?"

"Just a couple of miles south of Jupiter Shores. Why?" Diana asked.

"I'm going to go see my long-lost brother, that's why."

"All right. Family entertainment. We'll all go, make a day of it," Diana said.

Summer looked over at Austin. He was staring at her with such intensity it almost hurt. "No," she said. "I have something to do first. I mean, I think I do. Austin?"

He nodded, a barely imperceptible jerk of his chin.

"I have somewhere to go with Austin this morning," Summer said flatly. "After that I'll see about Diver and Marquez. Can I borrow your car?"

"Sure."

"But—" Seth began, glowering at Austin.

"I promised, Seth," Summer said. "Spend the day with Diana. There's a best-body-on-the-beach competition later, guys and girls. That should keep you both occupied."

Seth and Diana both seemed unnerved by her suggestion. "Why don't Seth and I go with you and Austin?" Diana said.

Seth nodded. "Excellent plan."

"No," Summer said. She smiled grimly at Austin. "Trust me on this. It's not the kind of place you'd want to go to."

16

Truth and Consequences

Summer parked Diana's car in the hospital parking lot. Austin hadn't spoken all the way there, except to read directions to her.

He leaned back against the headrest, eyes closed.

"We're here," she said softly. She shivered in the air-conditioning. She was wearing the most conservative outfit she'd brought, a black miniskirt and a cream crop top. She hadn't exactly planned on visiting a hospital during spring break.

"You want to go in?"

Austin shook his head.

"Austin, maybe it won't be so bad. The important thing is you're here. To tell you the truth, I'm kind of surprised you decided to come today."

"I guess I realized I couldn't put it off forever." He gave a shrug. "You were pretty tolerant yesterday. It was nice to just be with you and pretend I didn't have to deal with this stuff. But I knew it couldn't last."

"Your dad will be glad you came."

Austin looked at her as if he were trying to explain physics to a preschooler. "Summer, here's the deal with Huntington's. There's this tiny glitch on chromosome four, see, and it's like this DNA time bomb. When it goes off, you get depressed, suicidally depressed. Your brain starts to deteriorate. You can't remember your name some days, or the capital of New Jersey." He gave a dark laugh. "Come to think of it, I already can't remember the capital of New Jersey."

"Trenton."

"Oh, yeah. That's right. Maybe I have a few productive years left, then. Well, anyway, to top it off, you also get to jerk and spasm uncontrollably. Your body just says, 'To hell with you, brain,' and it goes berserk. Your face, your hands, your arms, your head."

"Oh, God," Summer whispered. "How awful."

"My dad first noticed it when he was playing the cello. He'd go to hit a note and his fingers would just sort of not listen. And then the jerking started. And the depression." He stared out the window at a stray seagull who'd discovered a half-eaten candy bar. "The last time I saw my dad, it was pretty bad. But my mom and brother say it's a lot worse now. A lot worse."

Summer watched the tears slowly form in his eyes. She slid her hand onto his thigh, and he took her fingers and clutched them tightly. "It's not . . ." His voice wavered. "It's not that I can't take seeing him. I mean, I know it'll be hard, but I can tough it out. It's that I . . . I'm afraid I can't see him without getting pissed. I'm mad at him. I know it's a horrible thing to say, but we never exactly had the perfect father-son relationship anyway, and now this is his big legacy? He wasn't around to teach me how to play ball or to give me crap when I was out late getting stoned or any of the usual dad stuff, but hey, he's leaving me the gift of genetic mutation." He gave a sharp laugh. "God, I know what you must be thinking. 'He seemed like such a nice guy. Who knew he'd turn out to be such an unholy jerk?'"

Summer stroked his fingers. She could feel the calluses from his guitar playing. "Actually," she admitted, "I was thinking what an unholy jerk I've been, worrying about my petty little problems."

"You?" He smiled affectionately. "I beg to differ. You happen to be perfect."

"Austin, you have every right to be angry.

This is a big, horrible thing to have dumped in your lap."

"Yeah, it makes a whole lot of sense to get pissed at my dad because he passed on crummy genes." He rolled his eyes. "I gotta go. I might as well get it over with."

"I'm coming, too."

"You don't have to come in. I know a lot of people have a thing about hospitals. It's enough that you came this far."

"Of course I'm coming."

He reached for the door handle. "I wish you could have met him before," he said softly. "I mean, he's not the greatest dad, but he's still pretty cool. Played a mean Bach. And he made killer lasagna."

They walked across the shocking sunniness of the parking lot into the hospital corridor. A graying woman in a pink-bibbed dress looked up Austin's father on a computer.

"Maybe after this I'll drive with you to go see Diver," Austin offered. "You and me, we'll make a day of it. Family reunions from hell."

"Let's take one reunion at a time."

"You're right," Austin said. "We should savor the moment."

They made their way down a long hallway to the elevator. Summer had been in a hospital only twice before, to have her tonsils out and to visit her friend Jennifer after she'd broken her leg skiing. But the smell was still familiar, alien and antiseptic. No matter how hard they tried to cover it up, it was the sharp, unhappy smell of sickness.

On the seventh floor they exited. There was a small waiting area near the nurses' station, with orange vinyl chairs and a coffee machine. "I'll wait here," Summer said.

Austin hesitated. He looked down the long hall as if it were a distance he could never manage to travel.

She pulled him to her and held him. "It'll be fine," she said. "When you see him, just think about the Bach and the lasagna. Let all the other stuff go for now."

He pulled from her grasp. She watched him make his way down the hallway. When he got to the door, he looked back and gave her a thumbs-up, and then he slipped inside the room.

When Austin came out an hour later, his eyes were red and his hands were trembling.

"You okay?" Summer whispered, slipping her arm through his.

"He knew who I was," Austin said shakily. "My mom and my brother told me he wouldn't, but he said my name, clear as day."

"I'm glad."

"It was something, anyway."

They walked to the elevator in silence. Austin

pushed the down button. "You know, it almost makes me glad my parents are divorced," he said in a weary voice. "I mean, it's not like my mom hasn't been supportive. She's visited my dad a whole lot more than I have. But at least she had a little emotional distance from it." He rubbed his eyes. "Not enough, but a little."

He didn't say anything more until they climbed into the car and Austin reached for Summer's arm.

"I want you to tell me something, Summer. Absolute truth, no BS even if you think it's what I want to hear."

"Okay. I promise."

"If it were you, what would you do? Would you want to know?"

Take the test, he meant. She knew what he wanted. He was looking at her as if she were possessed of some wisdom she knew she didn't have. It was a question for a priest or a parent or a best friend, not some girl you'd met on an airplane. But she knew if she told him that, she would be sorry.

"I've been thinking about it a lot, Austin," Summer said. "And it's not like I have the answers, God knows. On the one hand, it seems to me that if you want to keep hoping and not take the test, that's fine, as long as you don't let your fear change the way you live your life. As long as you don't avoid loving people and being as happy as you can and, you know, just living a normal life."

"A normal life," he repeated. "I don't know if that's possible. *I* can deal with that"—he nodded toward the hospital—"being my future if I have to. What I can't deal with is its being someone else's future. Someone I love. It would be so unfair."

"Not if that person loved you, Austin," Summer whispered.

He sighed. "I talked to my brother last night. Diana let me use her cell phone. His fiancée left him. She said all the things you're saying, and she still left him."

"So you're just never going to have a relationship again?"

He grinned lopsidedly. "I can still have casual, meaningless sex."

"But if you're going to turn into a hermit, why not just go ahead and have the test and be done with it? Then at least you can get on with your life." She hesitated. "I think—I'm not sure, but I *think*—that's what I would do, Austin. I think I would want to know."

Austin looked away. He seemed to be coming to some kind of decision. He nodded slowly. "I'm going to do it. Tomorrow I'll take the test." He turned to her. "Thanks for being honest and for coming with me. I don't know what I would have done without you."

"You'd have been fine."

"No," he said with certainty. "No, I wouldn't have been."

He leaned across the seat, cupped her head in his hands, and kissed her as though it were the last kiss he'd ever have.

"I know you don't want to hear this, but since we're telling the whole truth and nothing but . . . I love you, Summer. Completely and utterly and probably hopelessly."

"You can't fall in love in three days, Austin," she said lightly, but even as she said it she knew in her heart it was anything but the whole truth.

17

Fried Fish and Other Mysteries
of the Heart

Summer saw Marquez first. She was coming down a ladder connected to what looked like a tree house. She was wearing a tube top and shorts, and her wild hair was tied back in an unruly ponytail. Her legs, her arms, her feet, her hands—everything was covered in splotches of paint.

"You Tarzan or you Jane?" Summer inquired sarcastically when Marquez was on the ground.

Marquez spun around, clutching her heart. "Jeez, girl, don't go sneaking up on people that way!" She ran over and grabbed Summer in a hug.

"I'm not exactly the one who's been doing the sneaking," Summer said coolly, pulling away.

"I should have known you'd find me. I knew

Diana'd sniff out that card one way or another. Where is she, anyway?"

"It's just me and Austin."

"Hey, Austin," Marquez said, nodding to him. "I thought you were Diana's."

"Long story, Marquez." Summer's voice hardened. "So?"

"So?" Marquez said, glancing surreptitiously over her shoulder.

"So where is he?"

"He? You mean my guy. The guy. He's . . . not here. He's at work. How about I drop by the yacht later and we all party? This isn't really the best time, if you know what I mean."

"I know he's here, Marquez. And I'm really, really mad at you for lying to me."

"Man, you and Diana oughta open a detective agency. Starsky and Witch."

"I cannot believe you lied to me, Marquez," Summer said, her voice nearly cracking. "This isn't funny. You're my best friend and I trusted you, and you chose Diver over me."

Marquez looked pained. "It isn't like that. I just didn't think it was my place, Summer." She bit her lip. "He . . . he sort of thinks he let you down, you know?"

"He did."

Marquez curled a lock of hair around a finger. "Man, I knew this couldn't last. It was fun running away, but one way or another, stuff always catches up with you." She pointed toward a dilapidated trailer. "Behind that trailer are some cages. He's back there."

"Fine."

"Summer," Marquez said, touching her shoulder. "You can't change him. Diver's just . . . Diver. He's happier here. Isn't that enough? He wasn't happy in Bloomyburg."

"Bloomington."

"Like I said. You can't make him something he isn't. He loves you, and he loves your mom and dad. Can't you just let him be?"

"You would say that, Marquez," Summer said, unexpected venom in her voice. "You can't stand to deal with problems. Last summer, when J.T. found out he was adopted, you just couldn't deal with it. And now this. Your life gets a little complicated, so you just split and let the rest of us worry about you. You *would* think Diver's being here is a good idea. Maybe you two can just live out your days here in birdland."

Marquez grinned. "Don't tempt me." The grin faded, and she gave a shrug. "I know you're right. When it comes to bad stuff, I just get angry or I run. But I usually come around. I mean, I know I have to go back home and go to the damn art school and probably become a world-famous artist instead of a weasely lawyer defending white-collar crooks. We can't all be happy."

Summer almost smiled. "And what exactly is

Diver going to do? Stay here the rest of his life and be the eternal beach bum?"

"Jeez, Summer, who knows?" Marquez threw up her hands. "I'm lucky if I know what I'm doing two hours from now. Diver's happy right now. Isn't that enough?"

Austin gave a soft laugh. Summer looked at him, at his gentle, slightly mocking, understanding smile.

She felt her anger begin to slip away, but she held tight to it. She'd hurt too much to let it go now.

"My parents are talking about separating, Marquez. They haven't stopped fighting since the day Diver left. It's like they went through all this tragedy losing him, and then he comes back and they lose him all over again. . . . Never mind." She threw back her shoulders. "Back there behind the trailer, right?"

"Uh-huh." Marquez grabbed Austin's arm. "Come on, Austin. Let's you and me take cover."

"Summer?" Austin asked. "You want me to come?"

"No. I'll be fine."

She started off, then felt his hand on her arm. "One thing," he whispered. "Remember the Bach and the lasagna, okay? It worked for me."

Summer picked her way around the side of Peli-Ken's trailer. She passed several large plastic trash barrels. She steered clear of one in particular, marked *junk fish,* which reeked in the heat.

Two long lines of crudely made tall metal cages filled the sandy, cleared area in back of the trailer. Beyond it were palms and scrub pines. Birds, mostly sea birds such as pelicans, egrets and herons, filled the cages. It was messy and smelly and grubby.

It was not her idea of a good time.

She saw movement in one of the cages, a flash of blond hair, and realized it was Diver. Her heart lurched. He was filling a small children's wading pool with a hose. His skin was already darkening to a deep brown, and his hair was sun-streaked.

Summer hid behind a palm tree and watched him. He finished filling the wading pool and knelt next to a small white heron with a bandage wrapped around its middle. He was talking to it in his soothing, coaxing voice.

"Come on, guy," he was saying. "The water's fine. You don't know how lucky you are. Back in Minnesota right now all the ponds are frozen solid. The only way you could get around would be to strap on snowshoes. You got it made in the shade here." He splashed the water gently. The heron blinked a black eye at him, unmoved.

Summer shook her head in disbelief. Diver was wearing his battered old swim trunks, the only clothing he'd owned all the past summer. She and Diana and Marquez had bought him a

185

new pair at Christmas, a joke present for his Christmas stocking. And her mom and dad had showered clothes on him since the day of his arrival. Yet there he was, stubborn as ever, wearing those stupid trunks.

Her parents had showered lots of stuff on Diver—a VCR and TV, a home computer, not to mention toys he'd long since outgrown. Her dad had even bought him a football, hoping, she supposed, to make up for all the casual afternoon tosses Diver had missed growing up.

It had hurt a little, watching her parents fawn all over him while he'd grown more sullen and withdrawn by the minute. Summer had kept up appearances, stayed perky, tried to get everyone to talk during the long dinner silences. She'd done all the work, and Diver hadn't done a damn thing.

And now there he was, out of their lives, where he wanted to be. Alone. Well, not entirely alone, if you counted the birds and Marquez.

Diver picked up a ratty towel. He approached the timid heron, moving gracefully, infinitely slowly. "Come on, guy," he whispered, "the water's fine. You and me'll catch some waves."

For some mysterious reason, the bird allowed Diver to wrap the towel around its body. Diver carried it to the pool and set it down in the shallow water. Then he climbed into the pool himself, watching as the heron strutted gracefully along the edge. "Told you," he said. "It's not so bad, is it? You got your water, your sun, your bugs. Life could be worse."

He smiled, the kind of smile Summer hadn't seen in all the long months Diver lived with her in Minnesota.

"Maybe later I'll whip you up some of my famous dead fish à la Diver."

Summer grinned. The first time Diver had appeared in Summer's life, he'd made her a dinner of a fish he'd speared. Fried, nothing fancy. They'd just eaten it with their hands. It was the best fish she'd ever had.

She felt something warm and wet hit her arm and realized with a start that she was crying.

For a long time she stood there, hidden, watching her brother. Then, quietly, she made her way back around the trailer. Marquez and Austin were out near the road, admiring an old van with a pelican painted on the side.

"What do you see here?" Marquez demanded.

"A pelican on steroids," Summer said.

"Wrong." Marquez made a buzzer noise. "You see a magnificent work of art." She peered closely at Summer. "Hey, you okay? How'd it go? You weren't too rough on him, were you?"

"No."

"What happened? What did you talk about?"

"Nothing much." Summer looked at Austin. "Fried fish, with a little lasagna. Nothing much at all."

187

18

A Hot Kiss and a Hotter Fight

W e'll have to do this again sometime," Summer said as she parked Diana's car in the marina lot.

"Yeah." Austin laughed. "Like when hell freezes over."

"I'm glad you came with me to talk to Diver. Even if I didn't exactly talk to him."

"Likewise. I didn't exactly talk to my dad either."

They climbed out of the car. The afternoon sun was partially shrouded in clouds, and still the air was sauna-hot. At the entrance to the marina convenience store, three high-school guys were pouring jugs of water over their heads. Out past the docks, two girls were trying to catch the faint breeze on their windsurfers. After some feeble attempts, they both gave up and let the sails flop into the placid water. Summer looked for the Love Boat to see if there was any sign of Seth and Diana, but it was hidden by row after row of massive yachts.

"I've got an errand to run," Austin said. "I'll meet you back at the yacht. That is, if you don't mind my hanging around a little longer. I thought I'd go back to the hospital and see my dad again tomorrow. Then take the test."

Summer opened her mouth to say no, you really have to go now, Austin, you're complicating my life and I don't like all these feelings I'm pretending not to have for you, so please leave. But all that came out was, "Sure."

Austin slipped his arms around her waist. "There's one more thing I need to do before I go."

He leaned down and kissed her neck and made his way to her mouth and lingered there. It occurred to Summer that they were in the middle of the marina parking lot in the middle of the day and that this probably wasn't the most discreet choice she'd ever made, but she was too busy melting into the sun-drenched pavement to care very much.

Summer found Diana making a peanut butter and honey sandwich in the galley. Diana had changed into a shimmery blue tank suit covered by an Indian print sarong. As usual, even when she was being casual, she looked as though she'd walked out of a *Seventeen* spread.

"Hi. It's about time," Diana said. She held out half her sandwich on a heart-shaped sterling silver platter. "Hungry?"

Summer shook her head.

"I just love roughing it like this," Diana said. "So, first things first. You get my credit card?"

Summer climbed onto one of the red bar stools. "It's in my purse. Marquez promises she'll pay you back every penny this summer." She smiled. "She suggested that maybe she could do your portrait."

"I'll stick with cash." Diana poured herself a glass of milk. "So how was it? With Diver and everything?"

Summer shrugged. "I didn't exactly talk to him. I got there and . . . I don't know. It seemed kind of pointless. I know I can't change him."

"Hmm. Interesting. You're right, of course. Your brother is uniquely himself." She eyed Summer a little suspiciously. "So where's Austin?"

"He had an errand to run. Where's Seth?"

"He went down to the marina store to get some munchies. We figured you'd be coming back with Marquez and Diver."

"The store?" Summer repeated.

"Yeah, by the parking lot. So is Marquez coming by?"

"She said she'd stop by later, maybe. I think she's kind of happy just where she is."

"Sure. She's probably charged herself a condo."

"A tree house, actually."

Diana took a bite out of her sandwich. "Oh, well. It's only money. The truth is, and don't ever tell her this, I'm glad she's okay. So where did you and Austin go?"

"We . . ." Summer hesitated. She could still taste his kiss.

"Come on, Summer. I know something's going on, and to tell you the truth, I think Seth's worried, too."

Summer looked up in alarm. "Why? Did he say something?"

"You leave him to spend the day with me so you can run off with some strange guy, and you think he doesn't wonder? I mean, *I* wonder."

"Austin's dad is real sick, Diana. And he was afraid to go see him, so I went along, that's all."

"Really all?"

Summer didn't answer.

"Thought so." Diana sat next to Summer. "Look, I'm hardly someone who should be giving romantic advice. But Seth is madly in love with you, and he's a great guy, and I think you'd better get your priorities straight or—" She looked away, almost as if she was getting upset. "Or you're going to lose him to someone who knows how great he is. There. I've said my piece. Now you can tell me to shut up."

"You're right," Summer said. "I know you're

right. But don't you think it's possible to have feelings for two different people at the same time, Diana? Don't you think it's possible you could . . . do something that might seem hurtful to one person when you really didn't mean to hurt them, when you just really cared about the other person, too?"

Diana sipped her milk. "First of all, that was the most convoluted sentence I've ever heard, and I'm including conversations with Uncle Lester after he's had a few too many martinis. And second, Summer, I don't just *think* it's possible. I *know* it. I've been there."

"Really? When?"

Diana brushed her questions away with a sweep of her hand. "It doesn't matter. I'm just telling you that sometimes you have to make a choice, or else the choice will get made for you." She flicked crumbs off her sarong. "Now. You look like you need some comfort food. What can I get you? Peanut butter and banana, honey, or jam?"

Summer sighed. "I can't decide."

"Fine. You're putting your digestive fate in my hands." She looked at Summer with an expression of exasperation and something else, maybe even regret. "Never a good idea, Summer. I cannot be trusted. I'll take the honey and run every time."

Summer heard footsteps on the deck. She turned to see Seth coming down the teak stairs. He was carrying a grocery bag.

"Munchie man! All right," Diana said brightly. "I hope you got more Chee-tos. I can't get enough of those extruded cheese-food products."

Seth didn't answer. He turned to Summer. "We need to talk," he said flatly.

"Is something wrong?" Summer asked. "Did something happen?"

"I cut through the marina parking lot to get to the convenience store," Seth said. His eyes were black with anger. "What do you think?"

They walked wordlessly to the end of a long wooden pier past the yacht club. The pier was owned by the city, a relic of another time and place, but somehow the aged, creaking wood seemed more permanent than anything in the expensive marina nearby. A handful of fishermen were dangling lines lazily into the water. The air smelled of salt and fish, ocean smells that made Summer's heart quake.

"Seth." Summer touched his shoulder, but he just gazed out at the water. The afternoon shadows had lengthened, and the water looked darker, more ominous. "Seth, it's not what you think."

"Really." He spun around. A muscle in his jaw tightened. He looked to be beyond tears or simple anger. He looked betrayed, and the worst part, Summer knew, was that he had been. "It's not? There was my girlfriend in a major lip lock

with some . . . some stranger . . . in the middle of
. . . so everyone could see . . . so *I* could see.
God, Summer, if you're going to dump me,
couldn't you at least have had a little class?
Couldn't you have told me? Did I have to—to
see it?" He shuddered, as if trying to shut out the
memory. "You must think I'm such an idiot. I
mean, the guy's right there under my nose." He
blinked, coming to a new and awful conclusion.
"And that shower stuff when I got here—Oh,
man, he was there. Oh, man, you didn't."

"No, Seth!" Summer cried. "I didn't, I swear
I didn't. You know I'm not ready for that."

"I have no idea what you're ready for.
Apparently you can juggle two guys with no sweat."

"Seth . . ." She leaned against the wooden rail,
watching the waves slap haphazardly at the old
pilings. "It isn't what you think. I mean, it is, in a
way, but it isn't."

"Thanks for clearing that up." His voice
crackled with sarcasm.

Summer spun around to face Seth. "Look, I
can lie to you, or I can tell you the whole truth.
But the whole truth isn't very nice."

"Tell me," Seth whispered. "Just tell me."

Summer closed her eyes. "I did kiss Austin,
and it's not the first time either." Seth slammed
the rail with his fists, but she kept on. "And it's
true I'm . . . attracted to him, and I'm really,
really sorry, Seth."

He looked at her, his eyes veiled with tears. "Damn it, Summer, remember all that stuff you said at the airport, about us trying harder than other people, about how honest we are with each other? And then you pull this, right in front of me. Like I'm some dork who's so dense you can two-time him right under his nose." He gave a rueful laugh. "Well, I guess you had that much right."

"He . . . I'm not saying this as an excuse, Seth. But he needed me. And I wanted to help him—"

"You were helping him just fine out in the parking lot." Seth sighed. "And what about me? Don't I need you? Don't I count?"

"I guess you need me," Summer said, "but not in the same way, exactly. Not as much."

"Oh, fine, then. That makes it all okay."

Summer felt her throat tightening. He was right, of course. She couldn't defend herself. He was totally and completely in the right.

"Sometimes you do things and you don't even know why. It's like you're in the car, all right, but someone else is driving." She rolled her eyes. "I don't have any excuse, Seth. I just want you to know that I really do love you. I've always loved you. And I'm sorry."

He swallowed. "You mean you're sorry and you're going to tell Austin good-bye for good?"

She waited just a split second too long. "I think I got my answer," he said. Without another word he stalked away.

19

Diana Does the Right Thing
(for a Change)

M**an, you hide out in a tree house for a few days, and look at all the juicy stuff you miss!" Marquez exclaimed. She and Diana were winding their way through the evening rush at the seedy boardwalk carnival near the edge of town. The sun had just set, and the gaudy lights of the Tilt-A-Whirl and the Mad Mouse glittered against a blue velvet sky.

"By the way, I forgive you for ripping me off," Diana said.

"I said I'd pay you back."

"You are paying back. If you help me find Seth, I'll consider it total payback."

Marquez paused to consider some pink cotton candy. Diana grabbed her arm. "You can pig out later. First we find Seth."

"This is crazy. I mean, I thought I passed him when I was driving in and he was heading this way, but there are about fifty billion cute brown-haired eighteen-something guys around here, in case you haven't noticed."

"You said he looked at the van."

"It's got a pelican the size of New York on it. Everyone looks at Ken's van."

"I wish Diver'd come. We could use another searcher."

"He's still freaked about Summer, I think."

"You told him she was there?"

"I didn't have to. He knew."

Marquez stopped short and let the foot traffic move around her. "Diana, what gives here, anyway?"

"I'm trying to help Summer and Seth get back together. Duh."

"Yeah, but why?"

"Because. Because . . . she's my friend, Marquez. I realize that's a difficult concept for you to grasp—"

"Your idea of friendship is to say excuse me after you stick the knife in someone's back."

Diana yanked Marquez out of the flow. They stood near a shooting gallery. Lines of stuffed gorillas wearing leather jackets waited to be claimed as prizes.

"Do you really think I'm such a bad friend?" Diana asked.

"Of course I do." Marquez grinned. "But I like you anyway."

"You know, I do care about Summer. And Seth. I think they're really good together."

"So do I, but I don't see what we can do to help with this Austin problem. If I understand it right, that is, and I probably don't, since Summer was sobbing pretty incoherently and you're talking in riddles."

"Want a shot? Three for a buck," a gangly boy offered.

"Please." Marquez rolled her eyes. "They're totally rigged."

The boy shrugged and moved on.

"The thing is—" Marquez hesitated. "I mean, I would never have said this to Summer, but she's basically doing just what J.T. did to me. And face it, I'm a lot more resilient than Seth."

"Meaning you'll go out with anything with pants and a pulse."

Marquez ignored her. "I'm just saying Seth has a right to be angry. Maybe he needs to lick his wounds awhile, like I did."

"It's not that simple."

"It's always that simple. There's always a screwer and a screwee."

Diana hesitated. She could tell Marquez what had happened over Christmas. It would actually be nice to unload her guilt on somebody. But could she trust her?

Yeah, right. Marquez was hardly the soul of discretion.

"Come on," Diana said. "Let's try the rides. I'll do the roller coaster, you do the bumper cars. Meet you by the Tilt-A-Whirl in ten minutes."

"Can you lend me enough for a couple of tickets?" Marquez asked. "I love bumper cars."

Diana groaned.

"Can I cut in front?"

Diana batted her eyes at the blushing boy who had high school freshman written all over him.

"Sure thing, babe." He stepped back. "Be my guest."

"Thanks." She winked at him. "Give me a call in five years."

She tapped Seth's shoulder. He was standing in front of her. He turned slowly. His eyes were glazed. He had a lost puppy dog look that was awfully appealing.

"Diana," he said. His face darkened. "Did Summer send you? 'Cause if she did—"

"No. I'm here on my own."

"How'd you find me?"

"Marquez saw you heading this way."

He nodded at the coaster roaring past them in a wild S-curve. It was one of the old-fashioned ones, built on wood. It was very noisy and probably entirely unsafe.

"Wanna ride with me?"

"Seth, you have to go back. You have to forgive Summer. You have to make it work out."

Seth blinked at her. She wondered if he'd been drinking. He seemed to be having trouble focusing.

"How come you and me couldn't work it out instead?" he asked, leaning into her ear to whisper. "Like that night. It was good, wasn't it?"

He'd definitely been drinking. "Seth." Diana pulled on his arm. "Come on. We'll talk. I'll buy you a funnel cake."

He shook his head adamantly. "I've been in this line for hours. Come on. Stay, Diana. I need someone. Stay."

She sighed. "All right. But you have to listen to me while we wait."

"I'll listen on one condition." Seth pulled her toward him awkwardly. He kissed her hard, and she let herself enjoy the moment, even if he was kissing her for all the wrong reasons.

"Five years is a long time," the guy behind her said wistfully.

Diana broke away from Seth's embrace.

This doing-the-right-thing stuff was murder.

"Look. Here's the deal," Diana said. "Summer loves you. I don't. You're a friend, Seth, a nice guy, but there's no chemistry, okay?"

"I seem to remember things differently."

The coaster began to load. "Coming?" Seth asked.

Diana sighed. "Yeah, all right. What better way to die?"

They climbed inside the tin can of a car, and a bored-looking worker locked a bar across their waists.

"Here's the thing, Seth," Diana pressed. "Summer made a mistake. Fine. What you don't know is that Austin is kind of messed up right now and really needs somebody."

"Yeah, right."

"And what Summer doesn't know is that you screwed up just as badly as she did, maybe even worse."

Seth looked away. Across the boardwalk, the Ferris wheel turned slowly, neon arms glowing.

"How can you be so angry at her when you've done the same thing, Seth?"

"And what about you?" Seth demanded. "You were in that car, too."

"And I feel like crap about it. But I'm not quite the hypocrite you are. You have to be honest with yourself, Seth. Be honest, or . . ." Diana took a deep breath. "Or I'll tell her myself, the whole truth. I don't care what it does to my friendship with Summer. I'm not going to let her feel this bad about what happened with Austin when I know what happened with you and me."

Seth looked at her uncomprehendingly. The coaster began to crank up a long incline, groaning and clinking under the strain.

"That's like . . . blackmail. Why would you do that?"

"I don't have anything to lose. At least my conscience will be clear. Finally."

Slowly the coaster climbed to the top of the hill. Their heads were pulled back by gravity, away from the dazzle of the carnival area and toward the clean, simple glow of the early stars.

Seth slipped his hand into Diana's. "I do love her, you know."

"I know," Diana said, and then the descent began and the world was nothing but noise and wind and movement.

20

First Kisses and Last Good-byes

M arquez awoke to the smell of bacon and eggs and coffee, blended with the tang of the ocean. She stretched in her sleeping bag. Diver's shade was open halfway, revealing a breathtaking dawn.

"How did you manage all this?" Marquez asked, accepting a glass of orange juice from Diver. "And could you make a habit of it, please?"

"I cooked over at Ken's. He has a real stove. Eat quick or it'll get cold."

He sat cross-legged on the floor, watching with obvious pleasure as Marquez ate. "How come all this?" she asked between bites.

He shrugged. "I figured you're leaving soon."

The words shot through her. It was true—she was planning on going home the next day. School would be starting Monday, and she couldn't exactly stay holed up there forever, but still. She hadn't said anything to Diver yet. And it kind of hurt to think he was planning on kicking her out.

He patted her leg. "You can come back, you know."

"I know."

"On the weekends, maybe. It's not a bad drive."

"I know. It's just . . ." She tried not to pout. "It's just I feel like you're evicting me."

Diver combed his fingers through his hair. "Naw. You were going back, Marquez. I could tell."

"I see. What else can you tell, O great Diver, seer of the universe?"

"Well, let's see." He hugged his knees to his chest, studying the four-alarm dawn. "I know you're going to go to that art school."

"I see."

"And I know you're going to get over J.T."

"Preach it, brother."

Diver considered. "And I know you understood why I wasn't ready to see Summer."

"I'm going back there today. You could come. Diana's having a party on the yacht."

Diver shook his head.

"I knew you'd say no. Just figured I'd give it a shot."

"Maybe later," Diver said cautiously. "There's

always this summer. You and Summer and Diana are getting a place together, aren't you?"

"Assuming we don't kill each other first, yeah."

Diver nodded. "So there'll be time for me and Summer."

Marquez set her plate aside. "Sure. There'll be time."

Diver inched a little closer, so that he was directly in the path of the sun. He was also right next to Marquez—not, she knew, that he cared one way or the other.

"So you think I'll get over J.T., huh?"

"Yeah. You already are, a little."

Marquez smiled. She was, it was true. Not that she wasn't dreading going home. Or that there wasn't a big, gaping, annoying hole in her heart. Or that she didn't want to smear the name of that little tramp J.T. was with . . . but that was only in her weaker moments. Mostly, when she just sat in the sun painting, she felt pretty okay about life. Not like she wanted to drive ninety on the highway to nowhere, at least.

She gazed at Diver. He was so beautiful, so mysteriously unreachable. He'd helped her a lot just by letting her be herself, whatever that meant, for a little while.

"There's something else I know," Diver continued, still preoccupied with the sunrise.

"And that would be?"

"Never get involved with a girl on the rebound. It would be wrong to . . . to take advantage of her."

He let the words sit there. He was not looking at her. He might have been discussing one of his pelican patients or the latest in surfboard technology.

Marquez was pretty certain he was talking about her, but she wasn't certain enough to humiliate herself yet again.

"That's a good policy," she said neutrally. "Of course, if that girl was already recovering—halfway up on the rebound curve, sort of in the middle of bouncing back—well, then it would probably be okay to, I don't know, just kiss her a little."

He looked at her and smiled. Man, she loved that smile. It made her feel as if one way or another, everything in the world would be okay.

"Kiss her a little, you're saying," Diver said, his voice huskier. He moved a little closer still.

"Just a sort of warm-up kiss." Marquez swallowed. Her lips were dry. Her hair was a mess. She had morning mouth.

And then he kissed her, just a little kiss, and nothing in the whole world mattered, and everything in the entire world, it turned out, was definitely going to be okay.

Summer awoke to swollen eyes and a dry mouth. A brilliant dawn spilled across her comforter. She'd cried most of the night. She'd heard Seth return with Diana and Marquez in the evening, but she'd pretended to be asleep. She was relieved, at least, that they'd found him and he'd come back.

She climbed out of bed, feeling woozy. They had only two more days of spring break left. Nothing had turned out as she'd planned. Well, life was like that, maybe. She'd learned that much from Austin.

She hadn't talked to him at all after their kiss the day before. After her breakup with Seth (was that what had happened? Had they really broken up?) she'd gone to her cabin and stayed there. Austin had seen that she was crying and asked if she was okay, but she'd ignored his knocks on the door all evening.

Around midnight he'd come around one last time. "Summer?" he'd called through the doorway. "Diana told me what happened with Seth. Can we talk?"

She hadn't answered, and he'd left her alone after that.

Summer put on her pink robe and went to the door. Just as she reached for the knob she noticed a packet of some kind on the floor.

One-Hour Photo Lab, the packet read. She opened it. It was filled with photographs. Austin's Disney World pictures.

Mickey Mouse hugging Summer. Snow

White and Summer. Austin and Summer waiting in line for the Skyway.

There was a folded piece of notebook paper inside.

Summer opened it. For some reason, her fingers were trembling.

Summer,

I tried. I stayed up all night trying to talk myself into it, but I can't do it. The test, that is. I guess I'm just a coward at heart. Or maybe I just don't want to know the future. Maybe nobody really does.

Anyway, it's my life. I can deal with it. But it's not yours. Your life is about other things, Summer, wonderful things.

Work things out with Seth. He's mad right now, but I know he loves you. Not as much as I do, but then, that's not possible.

Thank you for being there for me. Perhaps someday I can return the favor. In the meantime, think of me when you wear your mouse ears. And have a nice life.

I love you,
Austin

Summer stared at the writing for a long time. Then she went through the pictures again, one by one. She lingered on the last one. In it she and

Austin were waiting in line at the Skyway to Tomorrowland. Austin had asked a nice man behind them to take it.

Summer was staring right back at the camera, looking a little embarrassed but laughing. Austin, however, was gazing right at Summer with a look of pure hope, in a way no one, not even Seth, had ever looked at her before.

She wondered if anyone would ever look at her quite that way again.

21

Forgiving, but Not Forgetting

I've been waiting for you."

Summer paused at the top of the stairs. Seth was sitting on the upper deck. He looked very tired. "Can we talk?" he asked. "I . . . where's Diana?"

"Still asleep. Come on. Let's go for a walk."

They walked along the dock in silence. For a while they didn't talk. The early morning sun warmed their shoulders. The wind was up, and the surf was churning noisily. Summer took off her shoes and let her feet sink into the wet sand.

"I thought a lot last night," Seth began.

"I cried a lot last night," Summer said.

"I was hurt, you know, to think about you with some other guy. Real hurt. But then I realized I . . ." Seth paused. "Well, I just want you to

213

know I forgive you. And if it's over between you and Austin, then I think we should try again."

Summer stared at him in disbelief. "You're just . . . letting it go? How can you forgive me so easily?"

He took a deep, steadying breath. "It's not so hard."

"I'm going to tell you the truth, Seth. Austin left last night."

"I know. I saw him leave."

"But if he hadn't gone, if he were still here, I don't know what I'd do," Summer admitted, her voice barely audible above the crashing waves. "I just don't know."

"It's okay, Summer. I love you. I can live with that. Let's just take it one day at a time from now on."

Summer shook her head in disbelief. "But you were so angry."

"I had time to think."

"If the situation were reversed, I don't know if I could forgive you this easily." Summer choked back tears. "Sometimes I think you're too good for me. I don't deserve you."

"Don't say that," he said fiercely. "I'm the one who doesn't deserve you. I'm the one who—" He stopped.

"What? The one who what?"

Seth gazed out at the ocean. "It doesn't matter now. Nothing matters except that I think we should try again, Summer. So it wasn't the spring

break we wanted. We've still got prom and grad-
uation and college. And all summer down in
Crab Claw Key. Three whole months of Florida
sun." He pulled her close. She rested her head on
his shoulder. "We can't change the past. But
maybe we can figure out the future."

Summer looked up at him. "I used to think
that, too. Turns out there's a fifty-fifty chance it
could go real bad on you."

"I'll take those odds. As long as I'm with you."

After a while they returned to the yacht. The
big waves sent cascades of spray onto the dock.
The yachts rocked like huge cradles.

"I still don't get it," Summer said when they
got to her cabin. "Are you making this easy so
you can torture me with it later?"

"Oh, yeah, I'll milk it for months," Seth said
with a laugh. Then he became serious. "Look,
we've got today and most of tomorrow. Let's not
ask any more questions. Let's get on our suits and
party with Marquez and Diana and just start over.
As far as I'm concerned, Austin never happened."

Summer kissed him softly. "Austin never happened," she whispered, her throat catching.

Summer closed the door to her room behind
her. She took a shuddery breath. After a moment
she went to her suitcase. She took out the two-
piece bathing suit and tossed it onto the bed. Under
a pile of T-shirts and shorts, she found the mouse

ears Austin had bought her at Disney World. She took them out and went to the huge bathroom.

She put them on her head. Another Summer stared back at her from the full-length mirror. She looked very sad and a little silly, and, although she might just have been imagining it, a little bit wiser, too.

About the Author

After Katherine Applegate graduated from college, she spent time waiting tables, typing (badly), watering plants, wandering randomly from one place to the next with her boyfriend, and just generally wasting her time. When she grew sufficiently tired of performing brain-dead minimum-wage work, she decided it was time to become a famous writer. Anyway, a writer. Writing proved to be an ideal career choice, as it involved neither physical exertion nor uncomfortable clothing, and required no social skills.

Ms. Applegate has written sixty books under her own name and a variety of pseudonyms. She has no children, is active in no organizations, and has never been invited to address a joint session of Congress. She does, however, have an evil, foot-biting cat named Dick, and she still enjoys wandering randomly from one place to the next with her boyfriend.